The thought of Simon anywhere near her bedroom made her break out into a cold sweat.

Not because she didn't want him there.

Just the opposite.

"I'm sure I'll be fine," she said firmly, tearing her thoughts from that traitorous path. She was not going to wonder what it would be like to kiss Simon.

Not. Going. There.

"I'm not helpless, you know," she said tartly. "I'm not the first person with a broken leg, and I won't be the last."

She caught a glimpse of his grim expression before it vanished. "Okay, then. Here's my cell phone number." He slid a slip of paper across the table toward her with his number scrawled in bold script. "I want you to promise me you'll call if you need anything."

"All right," she agreed, knowing she wouldn't. If she called anyone it would be her friend Rachel. Not Simon.

No matter how tempting.

Dear Reader

Thanks to all of you who wrote to me about how much you've enjoyed my Cedar Bluff trilogy. I'm always honoured to hear from my readers, and I'm glad you enjoyed the trilogy as much as I enjoyed writing it.

I'm thrilled to announce the debut of Simon's story. Simon Carter was just a secondary character at first—a friend of Jadon's—but soon I realised he deserved his own story. And deserved a strong heroine as his match.

Hailey and Simon both have guilty secrets in their respective pasts. Neither one of them is ready for a relationship when they literally crash into each other's lives. But soon they discover that only by working together can they free themselves from the mistakes they've made in order to fall in love.

I hope you enjoy CEDAR BLUFF'S MOST ELIGIBLE BACHELOR. And don't hesitate to visit my website and drop me a note.

Sincerely

Laura Iding

www.lauraiding.com

CEDAR BLUFF'S MOST ELIGIBLE BACHELOR

BY
LAURA IDING

Laura Iding loved reading as a child, and when she ran out of books she readily made up her own, completing a little detective mini-series when she was twelve. But, despite her aspirations for being an author, her parents insisted she look into a 'real' career. So the summer after she turned thirteen she volunteered as a Candy Striper, and fell in love with nursing. Now, after twenty years of experience in trauma/critical care, she's thrilled to combine her career and her hobby into one—writing Medical™ Romances for Mills & Boon. Laura lives in the northern part of the United States, and spends all her spare time with her two teenage kids (help!)—a daughter and a son—and her husband. Enjoy!

Recent titles by the same author:

A KNIGHT FOR NURSE HART
THE NURSE'S BROODING BOSS

This book is for you, Olga. Always be true to yourself.

CHAPTER ONE

HAILEY ROGERS walked into Cedar Bluff's emergency department on Saturday afternoon, fluffing her blonde hair to get rid of her helmet head.

"Hi, Hailey," Rachel, one of her nursing colleagues, greeted her when she approached the desk. "You're working arena team two today."

"Sounds good." Hailey had started at Cedar Bluff hospital about two months previously, but she'd worked in the emergency trauma center at Trinity Medical Center in Milwaukee for several years, so she hadn't needed long to learn Cedar Bluff's way of doing things. Rachel had been her preceptor but they'd quickly grown to be friends.

"I'll be right next to you in team three," Rachel said cheerfully. "So if you need something, or have questions, just let me know."

"Thanks." Hailey appreciated Rachel's sincere offer. The other nurses were friendly too, but most of them were married with children so they weren't exactly anxious to stop for a bite to eat after work, or go to a movie. Rachel was single, and she and Hailey had bonded after a particularly stressful shift a few weeks back.

Moving to Cedar Bluff had been a good decision for

her. She loved the homey atmosphere of the hospital and the town. Plus, her apartment was only a few miles from the hospital, making it easy to ride her bike to work every day.

Hailey glanced up at the assignment white-board and couldn't suppress a tingle of excitement when she noticed the physician leader assigned to her team was none other than Dr. Simon Carter. She knew who he was, of course. His chocolate-brown eyes, mink-colored hair and broad shoulders stood out dramatically, in her humble opinion, among the rest of the physicians. But in the two months since she'd started in the ED, they'd only worked together a few times and those had all been during her orientation, with her preceptor primarily interacting with him.

He seemed like a nice guy. And one of the few not married. Rachel had warned her that Dr. Carter didn't date any of the staff at Cedar Bluff, *ever*, but she couldn't seem to control her physical reaction to him. But it didn't matter because she wasn't in the market for a relationship either, so Hailey was more than happy to admire him from afar. She'd noticed all the staff called the doctors by their first names, but she couldn't bring herself to follow their example. Especially with Dr. Carter. Using his first name, Simon, seemed far too personal.

Heaven knew, it was bad enough that Dr. Carter's handsome face managed to invade her dreams.

Shaking off the inappropriate thoughts, Hailey quickly took report on the patients in her team from Alyssa, the day shift nurse in team two. With sixteen-month-old twin girls at home, Alyssa only worked one shift per week, and often that shift was a weekend.

"Hailey, do you have any questions?" Alyssa asked, when she'd finished her rundown. "Because if not, I need to go, I have to pick up the girls from their grandma. As much as my mother-in-law enjoys babysitting, I think it's getting to be a bit much for her now that the girls are walking."

"No questions," Hailey said reassuringly. "I can't imagine what it's like to take care of twins."

Alyssa laughed. "It wasn't too bad until Grace and Gretch learned to walk. They were preemies and a bit delayed in reaching their milestones, so they didn't figure it out until just a few days ago. Now it's like they're each on a different mission, heading off in opposite directions. Keeps us running."

"No doubt," Hailey agreed, ignoring a twinge of envy. Alyssa's husband, Jadon, was one of the ED doctors she enjoyed working with. They made a beautiful couple.

Once she'd envisioned a similar future for herself. Husband. Babies. Happily ever after. But not anymore.

Moments after Alyssa left, Leanne, the charge nurse, came over. "Hailey? I just put a new patient in room seven. Here's the paperwork." Leanne thrust a clipboard into her hand. Most of their nursing documentation was on computer, but the registration and consent for treatment forms were still on paper. "Fifty-five-year-old guy with abdominal pain."

"Thanks." Hailey took the clipboard and glanced up in time to catch Dr. Carter staring at her. The moment their gazes collided, he seemed to go still, and then tore his gaze away.

Had she imagined the flash of interest in his eyes?

Most likely. Rachel had confided that she'd tried to ask Dr. Carter out several times, but he'd always politely declined.

Not that Hailey was interested in dating him, the way Rachel had been. Still, it felt good to be noticed.

"Good afternoon, Mr. McLeod," Hailey said with a smile as she walked into her new patient's room. His wife was there too, standing next to his bed. Hailey quickly introduced herself. "Tell me what brought you to the hospital today."

The middle-aged gentleman grimaced. "We went out for lunch with my daughter, she's a sophomore at the university, and ever since we finished eating, my stomach has been hurting. The pain is cramping, and it seems to come and go. Do you think I have food poisoning?"

"Possibly," Hailey said, as she set the forms down and reached for a stethoscope. "But generally food poisoning sets in at least four hours after the meal. What did you have for lunch?"

"A steak sandwich and French fries," he admitted. His wife glowered at him and she suspected his wife had wanted her husband to pick a healthier choice.

"Hmm." She took his blood pressure, which was a bit elevated, either from the pain or because he had high blood pressure already. His pulse was tachycardic at 104 but his respirations seemed normal. "Put this under your tongue," she directed, holding out a probe for an electronic thermometer. After a minute, the device beeped. "Your temperature is normal, ninety-nine."

"Maybe it's just flu?" he said helpfully.

"Do you feel like you're going to throw up?" He

shook his head no. "Have you been told you have high blood pressure?" she asked, logging on to the computer to review his medication history. "Are you taking blood-pressure medicine?"

"No." He grimaced again, and she glanced back at him in concern. Whatever was going on with him, she doubted it was food poisoning. His medical history wasn't too significant for anything other than heart disease.

"Okay, Mr. McLeod, I'm going to talk to the doctor about your case. I think we may need to do some blood work, just to make sure there's nothing going on with your heart. And then you might also need some X-rays or CT scans to see what's going on in your belly. I'll be back in a few minutes, okay?"

"Can't he have something for pain?" Mrs. McLeod asked, a worried frown in her brow.

"I'll check with the doctor. I don't know if he's going to want to wait until we know what's going on with your husband first." She pulled up a chair for the woman. "Please sit down so you're comfortable while you're waiting."

"Okay."

Hailey made a few notes on the computer and then left the room to find Dr. Carter. Mr. McLeod didn't appear too sick, but her intuition was screaming at her that something more serious was going on with his abdominal pain.

The sooner they could get tests ordered, the better she'd feel.

Simon glanced up to find Hailey striding purposefully toward him. Keeping his expression friendly but distant took more of an effort than it should have. "Dr. Carter? I need you to take a look at Mr. McLeod in room two. I'm concerned about his abdominal pain."

He frowned. "Appendicitis?"

"Maybe, but he said he doesn't feel sick to his stomach and he's not running a fever. He does have a cardiac history, and ate a steak sandwich and fries for lunch." Hailey's expression was troubled. "His blood pressure is up a bit. One-seventy over ninety-two."

"So we'll do a full work-up, then," Simon decided. "Draw a cardiac panel, basic chemistry panel and blood count. If he has an infection, his white blood cell count will be elevated." He could feel Hailey's piercing blue eyes on his back as he headed for their patient's room.

He introduced himself to the couple. "We're going to do several types of blood test, to see if we can narrow down what's going on with your abdomen. Once Hailey gets your blood sent to the lab, I'm going to order a CT scan."

Hailey came into the room holding a fistful of empty blood tubes. "Should I put him on the cardiac monitor too?" she asked.

"Cardiac monitor? It's his stomach that hurts, not his chest," Mrs. McLeod protested.

"Yes, put him on the cardiac monitor," Simon agreed. He turned toward the patient's wife. "Sometimes chest pain can radiate to other parts of the body. We don't want to miss anything, so we're going to do a full work-up."

"All right," the wife agreed.

"I'll be fine, Myra," Mr. McLeod said, patting his

wife's hand. "I'll be out of here in a jiffy. I'm sure this is nothing more than food poisoning."

Simon suspected the gentleman was downplaying his symptoms for his wife's sake. He took out his stethoscope to listen to his patient's heart and lungs. Hailey came in close beside him, reaching around him in order to put the electrodes on Mr. McLeod's chest and then reaching up to turn on the monitor. He'd picked the wrong side of the bed, since the monitor cables were on the same side he was standing. Hailey's scent, something fresh, like the scent of the ocean, teased his senses. He eased away, as far as his stethoscope would allow.

When Hailey finished getting Mr. McLeod connected to the monitor, she went around to the other side of the bed, where the supply cart was located. Simon relaxed and finished his exam, verifying normal heart and lung sounds.

He moved his stethoscope to his patient's abdomen, expecting hyperactive bowel sounds. Instead, the normal gurgling sounds were diminished.

"Tiny poke here," Hailey warned. She deftly slid a needle into his vein, filling up her numerous blood tubes.

"I'm going to call Radiology to schedule you for a CT scan," Simon told him. "You're heart looks okay so far, but I think you may have something going on with your abdomen. A CT scan is the best thing to show us what's going on."

"Do you really think that's necessary?" Mr. McLeod asked skeptically. "I'm sure I'll be fine in a while."

Simon frowned. "Yes, I do think this test is necessary," he said firmly. Hailey lifted a brow but didn't say anything as she slipped out of the room, no doubt to send their patient's blood to the lab. He sharpened his gaze on his patient. "You may have appendicitis or something worse, like a pocket of infection or an aortic aneurysm."

"Hank, please." Mrs. McLeod was practically wringing her hands at the list of potential problems. "Don't argue with the doctor. Have the CT scan, please."

"All right, I'll have the scan." A mutinous expression darkened the patient's eyes. "But I'm already feeling better. I'm sure there's nothing seriously wrong with me."

Simon wasn't so sure, but since Hank McLeod had agreed to have the scan, he wasn't going to waste any time in getting it ordered. "Someone will be in soon to take you to Radiology," he promised.

While he was on the phone with the radiologist, he realized Hailey was standing beside him, chewing her lower lip anxiously, obviously waiting for him to get off the phone. When he finished his call, he glanced at her. "What's wrong?"

She let out a sigh. "Do you think it's possible Mr. McLeod has an abdominal aortic aneurysm? Everything about his presentation reminds me of a patient I had about six months ago back in Milwaukee. Same type of abdominal pain, same relatively stable vital signs, except for the high blood pressure, and even the same stubborn denial that anything was wrong."

Simon was impressed by her gut instinct. "It's one of my differential diagnoses, yes. And if he does have one, we'll find it on the CT scan. They're finishing another patient now, but they'll be ready for him in about ten to fifteen minutes."

"Sounds good. I'm going to give Jimmy and his mom discharge instructions and then I'll be ready to go with Mr. McLeod. I just need you to write out his prescriptions."

"Jimmy?" Simon had to think for a minute to figure out who she was talking about, and then he nodded. "Oh, yeah, the kid with the dogbite." He logged on to the nearest computer and quickly pulled up the sixteen-year-old's record. He entered in the medications and then printed the prescriptions. "Make sure he understands he has to finish all the antibiotics."

She chuckled. "I will."

Simon handed Hailey the scripts and then turned his attention to the other patients in their team. There was a twenty-two-year-old female patient with a severe headache that he was still waiting for Neurology to clear before he could consider sending her home. He figured she was suffering from migraines, since everything else had come back negative, but wanted the specialist to see her just in case.

Twenty minutes later, he got a call from the lab on Mr. McLeod's blood count. The gentleman's hemoglobin and hematocrit were on the low side, reinforcing Hailey's suspicion that he might have a leaking abdominal aortic aneurysm.

As Simon was on the phone with the lab tech anyway, he took all the blood-work information, relieved that the cardiac injury panel was completely negative. The patient's white blood cell count was negative too, which made the drop in his hemoglobin and hematocrit even more suspicious.

The minute he hung up the phone, his pager went off. He read the text message. *McLeod's BP is dropping, come to CT stat.*

Simon didn't waste any time heading over to the scanner, thankfully located right around the corner in the emergency department. When he arrived, Hailey glanced up at him, her expression grim.

"I told them to keep the IV in place. Do you want me to start a vasopressor to bring his blood pressure back up?" she asked.

"Yes, let's start norepinephrine titrate to keep his blood pressure above 90 systolic." He reached for the phone to stat page Leila Torres, the on-call surgeon working today. He quickly punched in the number for the CT scan, followed by a 911 so she'd know to come straight over. "How much of the scan were you able to complete?" he asked as he hung up the phone.

"Maybe half?" Hailey said as she pulled the IV medication out of the crash cart and hung it on the pump.

He crossed over to the reading room to look at the images. They hadn't quite been able to get half the scan done, but he could still see there was the slightest hint of blood leaking near the guy's descending aorta.

"What's happening?" the patient asked Hailey. "Is the test over?"

"Your blood pressure dropped a little too low," she explained. "We're starting you on some medication to bring it back up."

He caught Hailey's hand. "Tell Myra I love her," he said.

Simon caught the agonized look in Hailey's eyes. "I will," she assured him.

Leila strode into the room, glancing at Simon with an arched brow. "You rang?"

Simon pulled her into the reading room and indicated the worrisome spot on the CT scan. He kept his voice low so the patient couldn't hear. "The only abnormal lab test he has is a low H/H. He just dropped his blood pressure so we couldn't finish the scan. I think he has an aneurysm that's about to rupture."

"I think you're right." Leila was a petite woman with a hint of Asian heritage, and Simon had all the respect in the world for her skill as a surgeon. "I'll take over from here."

While Leila explained to Mr. McLeod what was going on, he called the OR to let them know an emergency case was on the way. Then he informed the radiology tech they needed a couple of transporters to run the patient up to surgery.

"We can't forget his wife," Hailey murmured, as they prepared to wheel Mr. McLeod down the hall.

"We've got it from here," Leila told them. "Go back to the ED. Tell his wife I'll talk to her when the surgery is over."

"All right." Simon stood next to Hailey as the team whisked the patient to the nearest elevator. This was the most difficult part of his job, giving bad news to families.

He turned and headed back to the arena. He was a little surprised when Hailey followed him into Mr. McLeod's room. Some of the nurses left the bad news up to the doctor. He appreciated her support as Mrs. McLeod looked up at them questioningly.

"Where's Hank? Have you finished his scan?" she asked, her gaze bouncing nervously between the two of them.

"Mrs. McLeod, your husband has an abdominal aortic aneurysm. What that means is that the biggest artery going from his heart down through his abdomen has a bulging section, where the artery wall is weakened."

"A weak artery is causing his pain?" she asked, her brow wrinkled in a puzzled frown.

"It's actually more than a weak artery, Mrs. McLeod," Hailey said. "This is a very serious condition that needs immediate treatment."

Simon nodded. "Your husband's blood pressure dropped while he was getting his CT scan. We started him on some medication to bring it back up, but we think the weak spot of his artery has started to give way. I'm sorry to tell you this, but he was taken to the operating room for emergency surgery."

"Emergency surgery?" Mrs. McLeod paled at the news. "But he'll be all right, won't he? I mean, you caught it in time, didn't you?"

"We acted as quickly as we could, and he has an excellent surgeon taking care of him." No matter how much he wanted to gloss over the risks, he knew she needed to hear the truth. "As Hailey said, this is a very serious condition. A life-threatening condition. He has a good chance of making it through this surgery alive, but there is a twenty-eight percent chance he might not make it."

"No. Oh no. Hank, poor Hank." Mrs. McLeod's stoic

expression crumpled. "Tomorrow is our wedding anniversary. Thirty-five years! I can't lose him. Don't you understand? I can't lose him!"

Hailey put her arm around Myra McLeod's shoulders and the woman sagged against her, sobbing as if her heart were breaking. Despite his resolve to keep a safe distance from his colleagues, a lump lodged in Simon's throat when he noticed Hailey's eyes filling with tears, several fat drops slipping down her cheeks. As she comforted the patient's wife, his gaze locked with Hailey's in unspoken, yet shared agony.

Hoping and praying Hank McLeod wouldn't die.

CHAPTER TWO

ONCE she'd managed to get the poor woman to calm down, Hailey took Mrs. McLeod to the family center waiting area, leaving her in the kind, compassionate care of the elderly volunteer behind the desk.

It was the nature of the emergency department to move quickly from one patient to the next. She loved emergency nursing but sometimes, like now, she regretted not being able to follow patients for longer than a few hours.

As she tried to get caught up with the rest of the patients on her team, she couldn't prevent her gaze from straying to Dr. Carter. Those moments when they'd stared at each other while Mrs. McLeod had cried in her arms had touched her heart—a heart she'd assumed was long frozen.

Cedar Bluff was so different from the big city trauma center where she'd worked before. Here, it seemed as if everyone took their patient's welfare more seriously. No, not more seriously, that wasn't the right word.

Personally. The staff took their patient's welfare personally. Maybe because the community was so close. Because they ran into each other at the grocery store, at church or even at the park.

"Hailey, I put another admission for you in room seven," the charge nurse informed her.

"Okay, thanks." It was just after six o'clock in the evening and she was somewhat surprised she hadn't had a new admission sooner. Not that she was complaining. The slightly slower pace made it easier to be thorough with every patient.

She enjoyed working with people, mostly because it helped her to remember that everyone had difficult situations to work through. Some worse than others.

She glanced down at her paperwork as she headed toward room two. A seven-year-old boy with a dislocated shoulder and possible broken arm. Her steps slowed as a chill snaked down her spine. One of the things every emergency nurse learned early on was to look out for the various signs of suspected abuse. A dislocated shoulder could be the result of a parent yanking on a child's arm, and abuse cases often presented with broken limbs.

Quelling her nervousness, she entered the room, mentally prepared for the worst. A young boy was lying on the cart, dried tears on his face. His mother, a pretty and obviously pregnant woman, was sitting beside him, holding his uninjured hand.

"Hello, my name is Hailey and I'll be your nurse for this evening," she said, quickly introducing herself. Deliberately focusing her gaze on the child, she crossed over to the other side of his gurney. "Ben, can you tell me what happened?"

The child glanced up at his mother, as if seeking permission, and the pregnant woman offered a strained smile. "Go ahead, Ben. Tell the nurse what happened."

"I was climbing the tree and I slipped," he said. "My arm hurts real bad."

"I know—we're going to give you something for the pain. But can you tell me what happened after you slipped? How did you hurt your arm?" Hailey sensed the boy's mother was frowning at her, but she kept her gaze on the boy. His story seemed a bit fishy.

"When I fell, I grabbed a branch, but it broke." He sent another nervous glance at his mother.

"It's okay, Ben. I'm not mad at you," the woman told him softly.

"But I wasn't supposed to climb the tree," Ben said in a wobbly voice, sniffling loudly.

"No, you weren't. But I'm not mad at you. Go ahead and finish your story."

Hailey glanced at the pretty honey-blonde-haired mother, acknowledging that she sounded sincere. But she wasn't going to let the woman off the hook yet. "What happened after the branch broke, Ben? Did you fall to the ground?"

"No, I didn't fall, I jumped. The branch didn't break all the way. I was hanging in the air when I felt my arm start hurting. When I jumped, I fell backwards on the same arm." His wide eyes filled with tears. "I'm sorry, Mom."

"Shh, it's okay, Ben." The pregnant mother sent Hailey a resigned glance. "It's not the first time Ben's had a broken bone. He's a bit accident prone."

Accident prone? The hairs on the back of her neck lifted. She highly doubted it. The way the child was so afraid of his mother's reaction didn't sit well with her at all. "All right, Ben, I need to look at your arm for a minute."

She gently palpated the extremity, reassured that there was a good pulse in his wrist. "I'm going to get the doctor to take a look at this arm, Ben. I think you're going to need X-rays. Do you know what an X-ray is?"

"Yeah. I know. It doesn't hurt." The calm acceptance in the child's eyes bothered her. No child should be that familiar with X-rays.

Hailey left Ben's room and crossed over to the closest computer, intent on bringing up the child's past medical history to look more closely at his most recent *accidents*.

"Where's Ben?" a male voice demanded. She glanced up in time to see Dr. Seth Taylor standing near Dr. Carter. The expression on Dr. Taylor's face looked grim. "Kylie told me to meet her here."

Hailey glanced at her patient's name. Sure enough, Ben Taylor. Was this the reason no one had looked closely at this child's multiple injuries? Because he was the son of a doctor on staff?

"I don't know, Seth. But calm down, we'll find him."

"Um, Dr. Taylor?" Hailey spoke up. "Ben was just placed over here in room seven."

"Thanks." Relief flared in his eyes as he headed straight for Ben's room. Dr. Carter crossed over to where she was standing.

"What happened to Ben Taylor?" he asked.

"Dislocated shoulder and possible broken arm," Hailey answered. "I'm worried about him. Hasn't anyone considered getting Child Protective Services involved?"

"Child protective services?" Dr. Carter stared at her for a few seconds and then started to laugh. "For Seth and Kylie? No, Hailey, you're way off base."

She bristled at his casual dismissal. "Oh, really? Just because his father is a doctor here doesn't mean this boy isn't the subject of physical abuse."

Simon's laughter ended abruptly. "You're serious!" he exclaimed, his eyes widening comically. "Come on, Hailey, I know Seth and Kylie. They're not hurting Ben."

"Then why is Ben so accident-prone?" She'd pulled up the boy's medical record. Six months ago he'd had a gash to his leg that was deep enough to need stitches. And another six months before that he was admitted for hypothermia after falling into Lake Michigan. And before that he was hit by a car while riding his bike.

Accident prone was an understatement.

"Because he's a mischievous kid who's probably looking for attention now that his mother has another baby on the way," he pointed out reasonably.

"Maybe." She couldn't deny his theory made sense, if Ben was telling the truth about climbing the tree against his mother's wishes. She glanced at the boy's history again. Falling into Lake Michigan couldn't be construed as abuse. Neglect? Maybe. But his mother hadn't been the one driving the car that had hit him. More neglect?

Or was she simply overreacting?

"Seriously, Hailey, you have to trust me on this. Seth

and Kylie are good people. They love Ben. They would never hurt him."

"If you're sure," she finally agreed. She didn't need Dr. Carter's approval to call Child Protective Services—anyone could make a referral. But Cedar Bluff was a small town and the more she thought about it, the more likely it seemed that if something like physical abuse was going on, others would know about it.

"Hey, don't be so hard on yourself," Dr. Carter said quietly. "Actually, you did the right thing by raising the question. Sometimes we see these people so often, here at work and out in the community, we don't even think about the fact that something horrible could be happening behind closed doors. Having new people work here is a good way to keep us on our toes."

He was being nice, trying to make her feel better. Surely someone with integrity, like Dr. Carter, wouldn't ignore a case of child abuse. "Thanks," she murmured. "You'd better go in there to see him. He'll need X-rays for sure."

"Will do." He flashed a quick smile before disappearing into Ben's room. She followed and halted in the doorway, watching as Dr. Taylor and his pregnant wife hovered over Ben with obvious concern.

A family united.

Feeling foolish about her original suspicions, and maybe a bit envious at their closeness, Hailey turned away to check on her other patients.

After the fiasco with Ben, the rest of her shift flew by. Several times she thought about calling upstairs to the intensive care unit to find out how Hank McLeod was doing, but other issues needing her attention prevented her from following through.

But after her shift was over, Hailey couldn't leave without checking on him. She didn't call the ICU but simply walked up the few flights of stairs until she reached the third-floor surgical ICU.

Worrying her bottom lip with her top teeth, she read through the names on the census board. She didn't immediately find his name and her stomach clenched, fearing the worst. But then she found him at the bottom of the list in the very last room.

She went down the hall toward his room, only to discover he was in the middle of a sterile procedure, a central line placement from what she could tell. She glimpsed at his vital signs on the monitor, reassuring herself that he was relatively stable, before she backed away.

Not an appropriate time to check with his wife to see how things were going. Maybe tomorrow she'd stop up to see Mrs. McLeod. As Hailey walked back out of the unit, she came face to face with Dr. Carter, who was apparently on his way in.

"Hi, Dr. Carter. Guess we're both here for the same reason," she said with a sheepish grin. She was impressed he'd cared enough to come up to check on their patient. "You can go in, but they're in the middle of placing a central line on Mr. McLeod."

"Ah, then I won't bother them." He stood for a moment, his hands tucked in the pockets of his lab coat as if he wanted to say something. "Hailey, stop the Dr. Carter stuff. You need to call me Simon."

Her eyes widened and she swallowed hard. "I'll—

uh—try," she hedged, stepping to go around him. "I have to run. I'll—uh—see you later."

"Wait, this is important," he called, halting her escape. "I'm not trying to come onto you or anything."

She sucked in a quick breath at his bold statement. "I never thought you were!" she said hastily, her cheeks burning with embarrassment.

Good grief, this was awkward.

Now it was his turn to avoid her gaze. Still, he continued, as if needing to clear the air. "The administration here at Cedar Bluff is working on a new initiative where we all work together as a team, keeping the patient at the center of all we do."

"Okay," she agreed slowly, trying to figure out where he was going with all this. "I'm all for making our patients a priority—why else would we be here?" And what in the world did that have to do with calling him Simon? She could feel her cheeks reddening at the thought of being on a first-name basis with him.

"Of course, we all do. But I think you're missing the point. The most important part of achieving the goal of patient-centered care is teamwork. Cedar Bluff doesn't want us to view ourselves as a hierarchical organization. Instead, they want us to have a team approach, where everyone has an equal say in what we do for our patients."

"Really?" She couldn't help the sliver of doubt in her tone.

Now his expression seemed a bit exasperated. "Haven't you noticed how big the first name is printed on our hospital ID badge? Or heard everyone calling everyone else by their first names?"

She nodded slowly. "Yes. But I'm used to calling doctors by their formal titles. It's a sign of respect. And I figured you all knew each other well enough to use first names, but I'm still new here."

He looked a little taken aback by that statement. "Not at all. I mean, I know some of the people really well but others I don't. Regardless, it's about being a team. Not a doctor versus a nurse, or a tech versus a nurse. A team. Got it?"

What he was saying made some sense. She reluctantly agreed, "Got it."

He looked relieved. "Good." There was another awkward silence and he cleared his throat and then glanced at his watch. "I have to get home, too. Goodnight, Hailey."

His expectant gaze forced her to respond in kind. "Goodnight, Simon."

His name sounded strange when she spoke it out loud and for a moment there was a simmering awareness hovering between them. After a few moments he deliberately turned and walked away, breaking the intangible connection.

When he headed for the elevators, she decided to slip down the stairs to go to the staff locker room.

In the privacy of the female locker room, she peeled off her scrubs and pulled on her skin-tight florescent striped biking gear, reliving those few tense moments when Simon had told her he wasn't coming onto her.

Had she given him the impression she wished he would? Or that she thought he was? Good grief, talk about humiliating.

He couldn't know that the last thing she wanted was a relationship. With him or anyone else.

"I can't believe you're still here!" Rachel exclaimed, coming into the locker room and interrupting her tumultuous thoughts. "Don't tell me you rode your bike today. I know it's spring, but it's freezing outside. Not to mention dark. Why would you ride this late? It's close to midnight."

Hailey offered a weak smile. "Biking is good exercise and I don't live very far. Don't worry, this fluorescent gear keeps me safe." Despite the budding friendship she felt toward Rachel, there were some secrets that were too dark to share, no matter how strong the friendship.

After all, she'd come here to Cedar Bluff to escape the past, not dwell on everything she'd lost.

"You're crazy," Rachel said, slamming her locker door shut as Hailey pulled on her bike helmet. "Truly crazy. Are you sure you don't want a ride home?"

"I'm sure," Hailey responded firmly. She pulled on her gloves and then opened the locker-room door. She had to shut this conversation down before Rachel asked any more questions. "Bye, Rachel. See you tomorrow."

"Bye, Hailey. Ride safe."

"I will." Outside, true to Rachel's word, the cold wind cut through her sweat-wicking biking gear. She clenched her teeth together to keep them from chattering. After deftly unlocking the bike, she jumped on and followed the familiar path towards home.

She'd come a long way since those dark days after Andrew's death. In the fourteen months that had passed, she'd recovered both emotionally and physically from the accident that had stolen everything that had been important to her.

But no matter how much she'd healed, she still couldn't bring herself to get behind the wheel of a car.

Simon mentally smacked himself in the forehead as he rode the elevator down to the first floor, putting as much distance between himself and Hailey as possible.

Idiot. How could he have been such an idiot?

I'm not coming onto you or anything.

I never thought you were!

Shaking his head, he strode out to the parking structure towards his car. He'd made a complete fool of himself. But at least Hailey would know that he wasn't interested in anything more than a nice, friendly working relationship. Teamwork, just as he had said.

He shouldn't have assumed anything, he acknowledged as he drove home. Just because Rachel Connell had asked him out a few times, it didn't mean every single female would.

Hailey was beautiful enough that some other guy would surely snatch her up in no time.

And why that thought annoyed him, he had no idea. Normally he couldn't care less who dated whom.

Simon didn't live far from the hospital, so he made it home in less than fifteen minutes. He walked inside his small ranch-style home and tossed his keys on the counter.

The blinking light on his answering-machine gave him pause. Most of his friends used his cell phone. He only kept the land line because of the need to be on call for the emergency department. He'd started out using just his cell phone, but he'd slept through the first call he'd ever received because the ringer on his phone, even at maximum volume, just wasn't loud enough.

Maybe his parents had called? He hadn't talked to them in over a month, he realized guiltily.

He pulled a beer out of the fridge, twisted off the cap and took a long drink before walking over to look more closely at the answering-machine.

Three messages, all from a blocked phone number. He frowned. Not his parents. Unless they'd changed to a blocked number for some reason? He pushed the play button.

The sound of a dial tone echoed in the room.

He deleted that message and played the next. More dial tone. The third one was also nothing but dial tone.

Three hang-up phone calls. All from blocked numbers.

Dread painfully twisted his stomach.

Erica had left hang-up messages. Especially in those final weeks before he'd finally picked up and moved, without telling anyone where he was going. Not only had he kept quiet about his true destination, he'd claimed he was moving to Arizona to be closer to his parents. He'd even gone as far as applying for an Arizona medical license.

No one, outside his parents, knew he'd come to small-town Cedar Bluff in Wisconsin instead.

Almost two years had passed. Surely Erica hadn't found him. Why would she even bother after all this time? She must have moved on with her life by now.

Hadn't she?

CHAPTER THREE

BY THE next morning, Simon had convinced himself that telemarketers had left the three hang-up messages. It was the only explanation that made sense. He needed to remember to update his number on the national do-not-call list.

He sipped at a mug of coffee, thinking about his plans for his day off. He found he was oddly disappointed that he wouldn't be seeing Hailey.

Stupid, since nothing would ever come of it.

He was through with relationships. After everything that had happened with Erica, he couldn't imagine allowing anyone to get close.

To this day, he still felt guilty for what had transpired between them. He'd had no idea she was the clingy type of woman when they'd started to see each other. She'd been a nurse working in the same Chicago Children's hospital emergency department he had been. The way she'd call him if she hadn't heard from him had seemed nice at first, complimentary. Deep down, he'd been thrilled to know how much she liked him. And she was sweet, too.

But then, when he'd tried to pull back a little, needing a little breathing space, Erica had got upset. She'd been so upset that he'd gone back to seeing her, thinking that perhaps he'd overreacted.

All too soon he'd known it wasn't going to work. So he had broken things off again. And then circumstances had changed and things had gone from bad to worse.

He closed his eyes for a moment, wishing desperately that he'd handled the situation differently. His actions had caused both of them to suffer. And then there was...

No. He shoved thoughts of Erica aside. Two years was a long time. She'd moved on and so should he. Maybe a tiny part of him would never be the same again, but he had created a new life in Cedar Bluff. New friends. And he was being considered for a promotion, the open ED Medical Director position.

He was happy with his new, if lonely, life. And he'd finally realized there was nothing he could do if Erica wasn't happy in hers.

Nothing he could do to change what had been lost.

While mowing his lawn, a job he liked for the sheer mindlessness of the work, Seth Taylor called him. He had to shut off the lawnmower in order to hear him.

"Simon, I need a favor."

"No problem."

There was a slight pause on the other end of the line. "I haven't told you what the favor is yet," Seth protested.

He chuckled at Seth's incredulous tone. "Doesn't matter, Seth. But go ahead and ask me, if it makes you feel better."

"I need you to cover my three-to-eleven shift in the trauma bay tonight. Kylie has to cover a sick call for the paramedic unit and I don't want to leave Ben with a babysitter as he's still having some pain in his broken arm."

"No problem," Simon repeated, glancing at his watch. He had a couple of hours until three o'clock. "I'd be happy to cover you."

"Thanks, man. You know I'll return the favor some time," Seth said gratefully.

"I know," he agreed. Since he was one of the few single guys on staff, he had less reason to need anyone to cover him, but he didn't mind.

Work was his salvation.

When Simon walked into the ED a few hours later, controlled chaos reigned.

Apparently several staff members were sick with flu, so they were working short-handed. Even with the tight staffing, he was surprised to see that Hailey had been assigned to work trauma with him.

Not that Hailey wasn't a capable nurse. She'd certainly proved herself with the McLeod case. But Cedar Bluff's policy was not to put their new nurses into the trauma bay until after six months. Hailey had come to them with trauma experience, though, and from a level-one trauma center to boot, so maybe that was why they'd made an exception in her case.

Secretly thrilled to discover he was working with Hailey after all, he crossed over to talk to Quinn Torres, the day-shift physician in the trauma bay, to find out what was going on.

"Hey, Simon," Quinn greeted him. "It's been steady all day, but nothing too overwhelming. The biggest issue is staffing. For second shift the trauma team is also covering team one."

Double duty. He grimaced at the news, knowing there would be delays with patients in team one if emergency cases arrived. There was nothing they could do, though, other than their best. "All right. What's the disposition with this guy?" he asked, glancing at the patient who was currently in the trauma bay, hooked up to a cardiac monitor and a ventilator. He noticed Hailey was there getting a report from Claire, the day-shift nurse.

"Fifty-eight-year-old guy with a GI bleed. We've dumped several units of blood and fresh frozen plasma into him, so he's stable for the moment. We're waiting on an ICU bed—hopefully should get one within the next fifteen minutes or so," Quinn replied. "They're moving someone out to make room."

"So are all hospital beds tight or just critical care beds?" he asked. Without open-floor beds and ICU beds, patient dispositions took much longer, causing back-ups in the ED. Not good on a day when they were already short-staffed.

"Just critical care," Quinn assured him. "And I think they're moving a couple of patients out, so you should be fine."

"Okay. Anything else about this guy I need to know?"

"Not really," Quinn murmured, glancing over at the patient. "We have an H/H pending and there are four units of PRBCs and four units of fresh frozen plasma on hand if you need them."

"Sounds good."

"Excellent," Quinn said, slapping Simon on the back. "Have a good night, because I know I will."

Simon had to laugh. "Is that your way of saying Leila is off tonight, too?"

"Yes, and Kane Ryerson is the surgeon on call tonight. Don't you dare page Leila unless you have a code-yellow situation," Quinn threatened.

A code yellow was a disaster call, something they'd never had to implement in time he'd been there. "Don't worry, we won't."

After Quinn had left, he went over to stand at the foot of the patient's gurney, taking note of the most recent vital signs flashing across the screen. Hailey was performing a physical assessment, her head bent down as she listened to his heart and lungs. His fingers itched to tuck the silky strands of blonde hair behind her ear.

He dragged his gaze away with an effort. So what if he thought she was incredibly attractive? Just the fact that she was a nurse on staff made her off-limits.

"Ah, Dr—I mean, Simon?"

He inwardly cursed when just the sound of his name in her voice made his gut tighten with awareness. *Get a grip! She's off-limits!*

"What do you need?" he asked, glancing up from the computer screen and keeping his expression neutral.

"His hemoglobin hasn't come up much—it's 7.8 now and was 7.5 before the blood transfusion," Hailey informed him. "Do you want me to start another unit?"

"Yes, that should work. Hopefully he'll be transferred upstairs to the ICU shortly," he decided.

"Sounds good."

Hailey smiled, but he noticed a strange wariness in

her blue eyes as she crossed over to the nearest phone to order the unit of blood.

He told himself to be glad Hailey seemed content to keep a professional distance between them.

Because heaven knew, if she were to come on to him, he wasn't sure he'd be able to turn her down as easily as he had Rachel.

Hailey eagerly transferred her patient up to the medical ICU, thankful for the momentary reprieve from being stuck in close proximity to Simon.

She'd tried to get out of working in the trauma bay for her shift but Theresa, the ED manager, hadn't given her a choice. The two trauma-trained nurses had both called in sick, leaving her to pick up the trauma shift.

Another reason she'd left Trinity Medical Center had been because she'd lost the thrill of working in a level-one trauma center. She liked ED nursing overall, but had told Theresa there was no rush in getting cross-trained to trauma. Hailey had planned on settling in for at least another few months before having to face her first shift there.

Guess not.

She could do it, she told herself for the fifth time. Of course, having Simon on duty with her served as a distraction from her past.

She didn't linger upstairs, as much as she wanted to, but hurried back down to the trauma bay, knowing another patient could arrive at any moment. Besides, there were still a few patients in team one to follow up on.

Her trauma pager remained silent, though, so when

she returned to the department, she left the tech, a new woman named Bonnie, to clean up and restock the trauma bay while she headed back over to team one.

She double-checked on the patient they were treating for flu. The poor woman had thrown up right after getting settled into her room, just missing Hailey's feet. Hailey glanced up at the IV bag, satisfied to see it was nearly empty. "How are you feeling, Christy?" she asked the young college student.

"Better," the girl murmured with a wan smile. "At least I don't feel as much like I'm going to throw up."

"Well, that's a relief," Hailey said in a light, teasing tone. "Good to know my shoes are safe. Let's have you try to eat something, hmm? I'll get you some crackers and white soda."

Christy wrinkled her nose and put a hand over her stomach. "Do I really have to?"

Hailey nodded. "If you can keep the crackers and soda down, I'll get Dr. Carter...er...Simon to discharge you."

"Dr. Dreamy's name is Simon?" Christy asked with a heavy sigh, running her fingers through her limp brown hair. "He's not wearing a wedding ring. Does that mean he's single?"

She chuckled and shook her head. "I'm not answering that, you'll have to ask him yourself." She left the room to get the promised crackers and soda, returning in less than a minute. "Here you go."

"Thanks." The girl's eyes brightened despite her pasty complexion and Hailey wasn't surprised when she heard Simon enter the room behind her. "Hi, Dr. Simon. I'm feeling much better after that IV you gave me."

"I'm glad to hear it," Simon responded, his deep voice sending a shiver down Hailey's spine. She didn't so much as glance at him, concentrating on disconnecting the IV tubing from the pump. "Looks like you're well enough to leave, Christy."

Leave? Hailey tossed the bag and tubing in the garbage and turned toward him. "I told Christy she had to eat the crackers and drink the soda first, to make sure everything stays in her stomach."

There was a slight hesitation before he gave a brief nod. "Good. I'll get the discharge orders started."

After Simon left, the young woman let out another sigh. "Maybe I should throw up again, just so I can stay longer."

"I wouldn't recommend it," Hailey said dryly. "A better plan would be to get healthy, and then come back to visit when you look smashing. Doctors aren't overly impressed with sickly patients."

"Good idea," Christy said, with such enthusiasm Hailey knew the girl was starting to feel better.

Barely three seconds after Christy Drummel had been safely discharged, Hailey's trauma pager went off.

She read the text message with a sinking heart.

Male victim, MVC, pulse 130, BP 80/40, long extrication, suspected chest injuries. ETA three minutes.

"Hailey?" she glanced up when Simon called her name. "We have a trauma on the way. Are you ready?"

No. She wasn't ready. But she nodded anyway, praying she wouldn't throw up the way Christy had. "Of course."

Hailey finished with her other patient's labs and then took her place in the trauma bay as the paramedics wheeled in the new arrival. The patient was a young seventeen-year-old male, who'd run his stolen car into a tree while being chased by the police.

He'd been wedged inside the car, to the point where it had taken the firemen over forty-five minutes to get him out.

The first glance at his pale and lifeless face made her blood run cold.

Not Andrew.

She kept the mantra running in the back of her mind as she concentrated on getting the new patient connected to the heart monitor. His vital signs were dangerously low.

The monitor began alarming. "I'm losing his blood pressure," she said sharply, with a worried glance at Simon.

Simon looked up at the monitor, his expression grim. "PEA. Probably a hemothorax with his crushing chest injuries. I need a chest tube."

Hailey grabbed the chest tube tray at the same time Bonnie, the ICU tech, did. Bonnie stared at her for a moment, and Hailey readily let go, realizing setting up and assisting with the chest tube was something useful the tech could do.

She vaguely heard Simon give Bonnie instructions on prepping the guy's chest. She hung IV fluids and performed a quick assessment, noticing the young man's abdomen was taut.

Their patient rebounded as soon as Simon placed the chest tube. Bright red blood came pouring out, though.

"Call Kane Ryerson," Simon said to Bonnie. "This guy needs the OR."

Bonnie headed for the nearest phone, but almost immediately the patient's blood pressure bottomed out again.

"He's bleeding into his abdomen," Hailey said, watching in horror as the patient's belly grew larger right before her eyes. "Simon? Do you see his belly?"

"Yeah. We're going to have to open him up here." Simon didn't look very happy with the prospect.

She tugged the peritoneal lavage tray from the bedside, but before Simon could get the guy's abdomen opened, his heart rate slowed and then stopped.

"No!" Hailey shouted, unwilling to believe they were going to lose him. She climbed up on a stool to start chest compressions. One and two and three and four and five. Breathe. One and two and three and four and five. Breathe.

We're not going to lose him. We're not. We're not...

"Hailey!" Simon's sharp tone finally registered. She stopped CPR and glanced up at the heart monitor.

Asystole.

"It's over," Simon said quietly. "Time of death, six-forty-two p.m."

She thought she could handle it. But without warning her eyes filled with tears. "Excuse me," she mumbled, nearly falling off the stool in her haste to get away.

"Hailey!" she heard Simon shout behind her.

But she disappeared into the staff lounge, shutting the door firmly behind her.

CHAPTER FOUR

SIMON followed Hailey as soon as he could, but by the time he arrived at the staff lounge she appeared to have pulled herself together. But her red, puffy eyes and stuffed-up nose betrayed how she'd been crying.

"Are you all right?" he asked, concern in his voice. He took a step forward, instinctively wanting to offer comfort. What in the world had happened in there? Did she know the young man?

"Yes. Sorry for running off," she muttered, avoiding his gaze and moving to brush past him.

He caught her arm to prevent her from leaving. Immediately, a sizzle of electricity zinged up to his shoulder.

Quickly, he let go and took a step back. What in the world was that? "Hailey, there's no rush, if you need a few minutes yet," he began.

"I'm fine." Her tense tone was not at all reassuring. "I shouldn't have left like that. I need to get back to work. And we have to make sure his family gets notified of what happened."

He stared at her for several long seconds. Logically, he knew it would be best to leave her alone. Maybe Hailey always reacted like this after losing a patient.

Especially a young man who'd had his whole life ahead of him.

And even if there was something more going on with her, it had nothing to do with him. So why was he so reluctant to leave well enough alone?

"All right," he agreed, stepping away from the door. She hesitated only a moment, before walking past him to return to the trauma bay.

Letting her go was harder than he'd anticipated. With a resigned shake of his head, he followed her back to the trauma bay.

The rest of their shift flew by quickly, but while they had several trauma calls, none of them were as serious as the young man who'd died.

Simon kept a close eye on Hailey, but she seemed fine as they cared for a seemingly endless line of patients. He sought her out at the end of their shift, intending to talk to her again, but she'd apparently left without saying goodbye.

He headed home, uncharacteristically frustrated that he hadn't been able to spend a few minutes alone with her.

The next day he locked his front door before heading outside to his car for his shift, ducking his head in the rain. A crack of thunder made him jump as he climbed into the front seat. He pulled slowly out of his driveway, the rain coming down in sheets making it difficult to see the road in front of him.

Lightning flashed and more thunder rolled as he made his way to work. He slowed his speed, peering through the deluge of rain hammering against his windshield as he headed to Cedar Bluff hospital.

Maybe they did need the rain after nearly a month of drought, unusual for April. But with the force of the rain coming down, flooding was a definite concern. Water pooled on the roads and he carefully rolled through the deep puddles to avoid stalling his car.

As he approached an intersection with a four-way stop, a cyclist came out of nowhere, not stopping or slowing down at the junction, instead racing across the street directly in front of Simon. Startled, and a bit freaked out by the fact that someone was crazy enough to be riding a bike in this downpour, Simon slammed on his brakes.

Too hard!

He wasn't going very fast at all, but his car started to hydroplane on the slick street, heading diagonally in a path straight for the cyclist. Simon's heart hammered in his chest as he gripped the steering-wheel tightly, keeping his foot firmly planted on the brake as the antilock brake system bucked the car, praying he'd miss the slim figure on the bike.

No such luck. He grimaced as his car bumped the cyclist with a soft thud, just loud enough to hear over the pelting rain.

His tires finally gripped the road, stopping the car abruptly. He grabbed his cell phone and dialed 911 even as he jumped out, heading for the cyclist who was sprawled on the pavement not far from the bike, which lay crumpled beneath Simon's front bumper.

He could barely hear the operator asking about the nature of his emergency over the sound of the storm.

"Injured cyclist, hit by my car. Send a paramedic unit. We're at the intersection of Grover and Howard. Hurry!"

Snapping his phone shut, he tucked it in his pocket as he knelt beside the crumpled heap of aluminous yellow cycling gear. His breath caught in his throat nearly strangling him when he realized it was Hailey.

Thankfully, a helmet covered her chin-length blonde hair, but her eyes were closed and her face deathly pale, despite the rain coming down.

"Hailey? Can you hear me?" He sheltered her from the rain with his body as much as he could as he felt for a pulse. Relieved when he found one, he turned his attention to the rest of her potential injuries. Her body was lying at an awkward angle halfway on her side, and he was loath to move her without a neck brace at the very least.

"Hailey? Open your eyes," he said, running his hands along the arm and leg that he could easily reach, trying to ascertain if she'd broken anything. "Hailey, please open your eyes. I need to know if you can hear me."

Her eyelids fluttered open and she groaned as she tried to turn over onto her back. She still had a backpack looped over her shoulders.

"Easy," he cautioned, halting her movement with his hands. He unhooked the backpack from the one arm and twisted it up and out of the way. "First, tell me what hurts."

"Everything," she whispered. Her blue eyes were wide and frightened as she gazed up at him. "But mostly my arm and the leg beneath me."

The naked pleading in her eyes did him in. He quickly

unlatched the strap of her helmet and supported her head with his hand. "Okay, you can roll onto your back very slowly but don't twist your spine or your neck."

She let out a whimper as she log-rolled onto her back, his hands cradling her neck and head for stability. He slid off the backpack, tossing it aside.

"You're going to be okay," he told her reassuringly. "A paramedic unit will be here any minute."

"Andrew?" Hailey whispered, looking at him oddly. A chill snaked down his back. Had she managed to sustain a head injury despite the protection of her helmet? "Andrew, is that you?"

"No, I'm Simon, not Andrew." He took her hand in his and she grasped it like a lifeline, her fingers cold in the rain. Her apparent confusion scared the hell out of him. "Hailey, do you know where you are?"

For a moment she looked confused. "On the road. We had a car accident."

Somehow he didn't get the impression she was talking about this most recent accident but a different one. Suddenly her reaction the day before with the young trauma victim made sense. The sounds of sirens split the air. He was glad, very glad, to know help was on the way.

"Yes, I was in the car, but you were on your bike." He held her gaze with his, willing her to remember.

She seemed to accept that, or else she couldn't hear him clearly as the sounds of the sirens were growing louder. The rain lightened up a bit, although they were both soaked through to the skin.

The ambulance pulled up and he loosened his grip,

intending to let go of Hailey's hand, but she tightened her hold on him. "No! Don't leave me," she pleaded.

He couldn't ignore the panic in her eyes. "I won't," he promised, feeling a little sick at the thought of how he'd made the same promise to Erica.

Different situation entirely, he told himself harshly. Hailey needed his support right now. Considering how he'd caused her injury, it was the least he could do.

Kylie Taylor was the first paramedic to reach them. He was surprised she was still working at nearly six months pregnant. "Simon! What happened?"

"I skidded on the road and hit her." The reality of what had happened made his throat swell with guilt. The roads were slick, but he knew he should have had control of his vehicle. Maybe if he hadn't stomped on his brakes quite so hard...

Kylie's gaze flashed with sympathy but she turned her attention to Hailey. "Oh, my gosh, she's the nurse who took care of Ben."

"Yes." Simon hadn't told Kylie or Seth of Hailey's suspicions about child abuse. "We need to get her out of the rain."

"We will, don't worry. She needs a neck brace, but first I want to check her vitals."

A second paramedic joined them, a muscular guy by the name of Mike, and soon they'd checked Hailey's vitals, fitted her with a neck brace and then slid a long board beneath her.

Simon wanted to help lift her up and onto the stretcher, but Hailey clung to his hand as if he were the only stable thing in her universe. The way she kept murmuring *Don't leave me, don't leave me* ripped his heart. He couldn't bring himself to let her go.

"I'm riding in the ambulance with you," he told Kylie in a tone that warned her not to argue.

Kylie looked like she wanted to protest, but she'd noticed Hailey's death-like grip on his hand and gave a brief nod. "You'd better get your car and her bike out of traffic first," she told him.

He fished his keys out of his pocket, knowing Kylie was right but hating to upset Hailey by letting go, even for a few minutes.

"I'll get it," Mike said, grabbing the keys. Mike yanked the bike out from beneath the car, tossed Hailey's backpack and helmet into the backseat and then slid behind the wheel of Simon's car. He parked the vehicle on the furthest edge of the road and put the hazard lights on. He'd arrange for a tow truck to bring them both back to the hospital as soon as he could.

The bike wasn't mangled as badly as he'd thought, and he hoped that meant that Hailey's injuries weren't as bad either.

Soon they had Hailey loaded into the back of the ambulance. Simon stayed out of Mike and Kylie's way as much as possible, while continuing to hold Hailey's hand. Her vitals were relatively stable, a little shocky but not bad. Being drenched in the cold rain hadn't helped.

Hailey didn't have any obvious signs of injury, but she easily could have several broken bones. They'd need a slew of X-rays to know for sure. She was dressed head to toe in some sort of biking gear that had protected her skin fairly well, although there were several holes in the fabric through which small, bloody abrasions could be seen.

He momentarily closed his eyes as his adrenaline rush began to fade. Dear God, the outcome of this accident could have been worse. So much worse.

Hailey would be fine. He'd make sure of it. And he planned on doing whatever was necessary to help her get through this.

Hailey stared into Simon's dark eyes, trying to keep herself focused on the present. There were lots of other healthcare professionals around her now that they'd reached the Cedar Bluff trauma room, and they kept asking her questions that she answered easily enough, but truly she could only see one man.

Her brain knew he was Simon Carter. Simon. Not Andrew.

But when she closed her eyes, she saw her fiancé's face. The open cut on his forehead starkly red against his pale skin, his eyes wide and unfocused.

Dead.

Her fault. It was all her fault.

"Hailey?" Simon's face hovered closer. She knew she was being totally irrational but she couldn't let go of his hand. If she did, she'd get lost in the nightmares of the past again. And what if she couldn't find her way back? "Are you sure your head doesn't hurt?" he asked for what seemed like the tenth time. Had she been confused? Lost consciousness? She couldn't remember.

"I'm sure," she responded. "I was wearing my helmet."

"All right, Jadon has ordered several X-rays for you. They're going to take you to Radiology now, okay?"

Radiology? Alone? "No, don't leave me. Please?" She hated the way she sounded, like a pathetically scared rabbit afraid of its own shadow, but just the thought of being alone made her shake uncontrollably. "I'm s-sorry," she whispered, her teeth chattering as the sudden coldness overwhelmed her. "B-but if you could just s-stay with me for a while longer..."

"She's cold," Simon said, a harsh edge to his voice. "Someone get her a warm blanket." Then his face appeared in her line of vision, and he was gazing down at her with a relaxed smile. "I'll stay right beside you the entire time," he vowed. "I promise I won't leave you alone, Hailey, not for a minute."

"Thank you," she whispered. The warm blanket that Bonnie threw over her felt wonderful, but she was more grateful for Simon's unwavering acceptance of her irrational fear than anything else.

She should have felt embarrassed, knowing these people she worked with had seen her nearly naked, having cut off her biking gear before covering her with a hospital gown. But she couldn't seem to care. Simon had kept his gaze locked on hers the entire time.

It seemed they were in Radiology for ever, getting X-rays of her entire body. She couldn't suppress a twinge of guilt at how Simon had remained true to his word, staying right beside her and holding her hand, wearing a lead apron to help protect himself against being overly exposed to the various X-rays.

She needed to get a grip here and stop clinging to the poor man. With the rain in her eyes, fogging up her goggles, she hadn't even seen his car. Normally she was a defensive cyclist. But today she'd been preoccupied.

She needed to let him know the accident wasn't his fault.

As soon as she could find the strength to relinquish her hold on his hand.

"Tibia fracture?" she overheard Simon say as the radiologist came out to talk to him. "Nothing else? Are you absolutely positive?"

"Yep. She'll have plenty of bruises, I'm sure, but overall she's incredibly lucky," the radiologist allowed. "I've sent them to Jadon to see, but you can read them for yourself, if you like. Everything is clean, including her spine."

"Thank God," Simon murmured. He gave the radiologist a nod and then swung his gaze down to hers. "Hailey, I need to tell you that you have a non-displaced right tibia fracture. No other broken bones, thankfully, but we'll need to get your right leg in a cast. After that, all we need to do is watch you for a while to rule out any internal bleeding."

Considering her minor injury, she felt even worse at how she'd been acting. For heaven's sake, she was an ED nurse—a measly broken leg was nothing. "I'm sure I'll be fine. My muscles ache a bit, but I don't have any other sharp pains. Mostly bruises, like he said."

"I'll feel better once we get a CT scan of your head and abdomen," Simon said, his expression grim. "There was another trauma who was already in the CT scanner so we decided to go with regular X-rays first."

For a moment the panic at being alone hovered, but

she thrust it away with steely determination. Enough already. She was not going to expose Simon to any more radiation. Somehow she'd deal with the CT scan, and whatever other tests and treatments she needed, alone.

Or she could ask Simon to find Rachel. Surely Rachel wouldn't mind coming down to sit with her for a while. Although she'd no doubt give Hailey a piece of her mind for riding her bike to work in a thunderstorm.

Her bike. Heavens, how was she going to ride her bike with a broken leg? For that matter, how was she going to work with a broken leg?

She took a deep breath and tried to keep calm. There was no point in worrying over things she couldn't change. She needed to pull herself together, starting right now.

Two transporters arrived to push her gurney back to the ED, while Simon walked alongside.

"Thank you," she said finally, prising her fingers from his hand. She forced a smile she was far from feeling. "I'll be fine. I'm sorry I got so worked up over nothing." She wondered if her face was as red as it felt. She couldn't imagine what he thought of her. First the awkwardness last night and now this. Talk about adding insult to injury. "Honestly, I'm usually not so pathetic in a crisis."

"Don't," Simon said in a low, rough tone. She'd let go of his hand but he'd kept his fingers lightly wrapped around hers, refusing to relinquish the skin-to-skin contact. "You have nothing to apologise for, Hailey. I'm the one who needs to apologise to you."

For a moment she was confused. "For what?"

"Don't you remember?" His face wore an incredulous expression. "I'm the driver of the car that hit you. I could have killed you, Hailey."

CHAPTER FIVE

"No!" HAILEY stared up at Simon earnestly, hating the shadow of self-loathing in his eyes. She needed to make him understand. "It was my fault, not yours. I couldn't see anything in the rain. I never saw your car."

"Don't bother trying to let me off the hook," Simon said grimly, in a low tone. "It's always the driver's fault when losing control of the vehicle." He shook his head impatiently. "Why am I arguing with a concussed woman?"

She scowled. "I don't have a concussion. I was wearing my helmet."

"You were confused at the scene," he said firmly. "I'm reserving judgement until we see the results of your scans."

She didn't remember being confused at the scene, except for the flashback. Had she said something weird to Simon? She didn't have time to ask because the transporters wheeled her into the CT scan.

"Hi, there," the tech greeted her cheerfully. "We're going to move you onto this table here, okay?" The radiology assistant paused and then asked, "You're not pregnant, are you?"

"No, I'm not pregnant." She could feel her face

flushing again with embarrassment. It was a legitimate question, but that didn't mean she had to like it. There was an odd expression on Simon's face when she tugged on her hand, the one he still held captive. "You can let go now. I'm fine."

The enigmatic look in his eyes was a bit confusing, but eventually something in her gaze must have reassured him because he released her hand slowly, before stepping back. She looked over at the radiology tech. "I'm ready."

"Be careful of her right leg," Simon warned as the radiology tech and the two transporters began to slide her from the gurney over to the CT table. They managed to get the task accomplished without jostling her leg too much, although she couldn't help wincing a bit as the throbbing in her right leg made itself known.

How she'd ignored the pain up until now was a miracle. Must have been the effect of holding onto Simon's hand.

She closed her eyes, pushing away the ridiculous thought as the machine whirled and the table began to slowly move her through the opening. First they took pictures of her head and then of her chest and abdomen. Overall the entire process took a good twenty minutes, and she fully expected Simon would be gone once the scan was finished.

But he surprised her by staying. Hovering at her side again, as the staff slid her back onto the gurney.

No doubt he'd stuck around out of guilt. And because she'd clung to him like a limpet. She was such a wimp.

"We need the radiologist to review the scans for the

official read," Simon informed her. "But I didn't see anything major. No bleeding in your head, chest or abdomen."

She forced a smile. "Good. See? I told you I was fine."

He scowled, but didn't say anything else as the two transporters took her back to the emergency department. Based on the nature of her seemingly minor injuries, they took her into one of the rooms in the arena, rather than back to the trauma room. Simon took a few minutes to make a phone call out in the hall, before following her into the room.

"Thanks for staying, Simon," she said finally. "But you must have much better things to do than to hang around here. I'm sure you're probably working tonight." Actually, she knew he was working second shift because she'd checked the schedule before going home last evening.

But how could she tell Simon she'd been preoccupied with thoughts of working with him again, when she should have been paying attention to her surroundings on the slick roads?

Guilt threatened to choke her again. She really needed to learn to concentrate while traveling.

"I was scheduled to work but Jadon is going to stick around for a couple of hours until Seth can get here to cover my shift."

For long moments she stared at him. Was he still feeling guilty about hitting her? "I told you, I'm fine, Simon. I don't want you to rearrange your schedule just for me."

"Trust me, I'm doing this for myself as much as I'm

doing it for you," he corrected in a low voice. He pushed his fingers through his hair. "It's not every day I hit a cyclist."

She suppressed another sigh. "You're going to make me feel bad if you keep up that attitude," she warned. "I highly doubt you were expecting to find anyone riding in the storm in the first place, right?"

She saw the flash of acknowledgment in his gaze before a knock at her door interrupted them. An older gentleman poked his head inside the door. "Hello. May I come in?"

"Sure." She stared at him, thinking he looked familiar, but she couldn't quite remember his name.

"I'm Dr. Maxwell," he said kindly, coming inside and dragging a plaster cart behind him. He reached over to take her hand. "I'm here to examine and cast your right leg."

Oh, yes, Dr. Maxwell was the orthopedic surgeon, she remembered now. Simon eased back, obviously willing to give her some privacy. "I'll check back with you in a little while," he assured her.

"Thanks," she murmured. There was no need for Simon to check back with her, but she suspected nothing she could say was going to convince him of that.

Guilt. Wasn't she all too familiar with the emotion?

"So I hear you had a run-in with a car?" The older doctor gently smoothed his hands over her right leg and she couldn't hide a wince. "Luckily for you, this is a clean fracture and shouldn't put you out of commission for too long."

She bit her lip anxiously, mentally calculating how much money she had in her savings account. Not nearly enough to be off work for any length of time. She needed to talk to her boss, Theresa, as soon as possible. "How long?" she asked, bracing herself for the news.

"Well, I'd like you to stay off it completely for two weeks. You'll need to follow up with me in the clinic and if the bone is healing well, we should be able to switch over to a walking cast."

Two weeks? She tried not to let her dismay show. Two weeks would seem like for ever, sitting around at home. There was no way in the world she was going to be able to ride her bike with a cast. "But I can get around on crutches, right?"

"Absolutely," he assured her. "We're going to put a cast on this leg, from your knee down to your foot." He turned toward the cart and pulled out a stocking. "How are you doing as far as pain medication?"

"I'm fine," she said, lying through her teeth. She wasn't exactly fine, but she didn't want to take anything that would make her groggy. Or loopy. She was afraid the flashbacks would return.

Besides, narcotics made her itch.

The orthopedic doctor chatted while he applied the cast, probably trying to divert her attention from the task at hand. The pain quadrupled when he lifted her leg off the bed to wrap the wet cast material around it. She gritted her teeth, feeling faint as waves of pain washed over her.

She was immensely relieved when he gently eased her leg back down on the pillow. He checked the circulation in her toes and the pulse behind her knee one last time before declaring he was finished.

"Remember, come back to see me in two weeks, sooner if you're having any problems, all right?"

"I won't forget," she promised weakly, wiping the sheen of perspiration from her upper lip. Maybe she'd have to break down and take some pain medication after all, because the throbbing had only become horrendously worse instead of better.

Dr. Maxwell left and she closed her eyes, breathing deeply in an effort to get a grip on the pain.

"Hailey!" Her eyes flew open at the sound of her name. Rachel rushed into the room, with Simon following behind her. "My God, Hailey, what happened?"

"I ran into Simon on my bike," she said quickly pre-empting his response. "I couldn't see a thing. My goggles were totally fogged up."

"You rode to work in a thunderstorm?" Rachel said, her tone rising incredulously. "A car crash was the least of your worries. What if you'd been struck by lightning? Why on earth didn't you call me? I would have driven you to work even on my day off."

In hindsight, that would have been a smarter thing to do. But she'd already dodged Rachel's questions regarding her decision to ride her bike everywhere. She hadn't wanted to outright lie to her friend.

She'd come to Cedar Bluff to forget the past. Not be reminded of it on a daily basis. Yet here she was, reliving it anyway.

"I should have called," she acknowledged, glancing at Simon. "See? This really was my fault. Even Rachel thinks I'm stupid."

"Why were you riding your bike in the thunderstorm?" Simon asked, his intense gaze unwavering. "Did your car break down?"

She hesitated, not sure how to answer that one. But she needn't have worried.

Rachel rolled her eyes. "Car? What car? Hailey doesn't *own* a car. She rides everywhere on that bike of hers. And I mean everywhere!"

Simon couldn't believe what he was hearing. Hailey didn't own a car? Because she couldn't afford one? Had to be. He couldn't imagine anyone not wanting the ease of car transportation.

"Thanks for blabbing, Rach," Hailey muttered.

Simon lifted a brow, but let the comment go. "I'll drive you home," he announced.

Hailey's eyes widened. "That's not necessary," she started to say.

But Rachel cut her off. "Yes, it is necessary. I'm covering your shift, so I can't drive you home. And I don't care what you say, there's no way on earth you're going to be able to crutch-walk three miles to your apartment."

Simon bit back a curse at the image. What was wrong with her? Why was Hailey being so stubborn? "I'm driving you home," he said again, in a steely tone that left no room for argument.

Rachel flashed an odd glance at him, but then nodded. "Good. So that's settled." She turned back to Hailey. "I have to go take care of my patients, but call me later, okay?"

"Okay," Hailey agreed, resigned acceptance in her tone.

When Rachel left, a heavy silence hung over the

room. Simon scrubbed his hand over his jaw, searching for something to say.

She shifted her weight on the cart, sucking in a quick breath when she moved her right leg. Her face was whiter than the hospital bed sheets and when he looked closely, he saw a faint sheen of sweat covering her brow.

"Have you taken anything for the pain?" he asked. She looked awful. Worse than awful.

"No." She worried her lower lip between her teeth in a habit he shouldn't have found endearing but did. "I was thinking of asking for some ibuprofen but I don't want to take it on an empty stomach."

Ibuprofen? For a broken leg? "Do you have something against narcotics?" he asked warily.

She gave a small shrug. "They make me itch."

Since itching could be an early sign of an allergic reaction, he sighed and nodded. "Okay, there is non-narcotic pain medication too, you know. I'll talk to Jadon, see what he's ordered."

"I'd really rather wait until I get home," she said, when he moved toward the door.

"Getting in and out of a car and then from the car into your apartment is going to hurt," he told her bluntly. "I suggest you have something now."

He took it as a good sign that she didn't argue. Taking control of the situation, Simon arranged for her to get a dose of the medication now and a prescription filled by the outpatient pharmacy here at the hospital. Jadon was happy to write her discharge orders after getting the official all-clear on her CT scans from the radiologist.

Simon still couldn't believe Hailey didn't own a car,

but didn't ask about it as he pushed her wheelchair out to the ED surface parking lot, where the towing company had left his vehicle. The tow-truck operator had told him there wasn't a scratch on his car. That made him feel even more guilty.

Of course Hailey and her bike had sustained the brunt of the damage.

The torrential rain had tapered off to an annoying drizzle. Hailey was wearing a pair of scrubs Rachel had dug out of her locker and a borrowed windbreaker to help keep her warm.

After setting the brakes on the wheelchair, he went over to open the passenger door. Hailey didn't wait for his help, though. She pushed herself up on her good leg, balancing precariously as she reached around for her crutches.

He muttered an oath under his breath and tucked his arm around her waist. "I've got you," he murmured. "Don't worry about the crutches for now. All you need to do is to pivot around and I'll get you into the car."

Her breath was warm and moist against his neck as he held her close, supporting the bulk of her weight so she wouldn't have to do anything.

Hailey reached up to wrap her arm more firmly around his shoulder, bringing her body even closer to his. He could feel every sensual curve pressed against him, and he froze, alarm bells clamoring in the back of his mind.

Holding her close like this felt good. Sinfully good. For a moment he was tempted to breathe deeply, basking in her fresh scent.

He yanked his mind away from that train of thought.

Hailey would not appreciate knowing he was thinking along these lines when she was in terrible pain from a broken leg he'd caused, no matter what she'd claimed about who had been to blame.

Grimly, he concentrated on the task at hand. Somehow he managed to swing her around so that she was close to the passenger door. He ignored his physical response to her nearness, tucking one hand behind her thigh to support her casted leg and the other around her shoulders as she lowered herself into the passenger seat.

"Thanks, I have it now," she murmured breathlessly. He could see she was breathing rapidly, as if she'd run a marathon instead of simply getting settled in the car. The way she avoided his gaze made him think she was embarrassed.

Hell, if anyone should be embarrassed, it should be him. For thinking with the lower part of his anatomy instead of his brain. Hadn't he learned his lesson the hard way?

He tucked the crutches into the backseat. After closing the door, he walked around to the driver's side, momentarily turning his face up to the rain, welcoming the coolness.

He needed to stay in control. No matter how his body managed to betray him, he would not act on his feelings.

Not now.

Not ever.

As he slid behind the wheel and started the car, Simon did his best to think of Hailey as a patient. She'd latched her seat belt, he saw with approval, but had leaned back against the headrest, her eyes closed.

"Are you okay?" he asked, as he backed out of the parking space. He knew she had the prescription bottle of non-narcotic pain pills tucked in the pocket of her windbreaker.

"Fine," she whispered, keeping her eyes closed.

He could appreciate how exhausted she must be, but he needed to know where to go. "Hailey? What street do you live on?"

She turned her head and cracked one eye open to look at him. "The Rose Glen apartment building, off Howard."

"Got it," he said, turning right to head in that direction.

Hailey didn't move, but her hands were clasped tightly in her lap, so he knew she wasn't sleeping.

No, not sleeping. More likely, she was fighting the pain. It would take a while for the full effect of the pain medication to work.

He pulled into the parking lot behind the apartment complex, somewhat relieved to notice it was only a two-story building. He was willing to wager, however, that Hailey lived on the second floor.

"I can do it," she said testily, but in the end she needed his arm to help her get out of the car. He reached for the crutches, offering them to her once she was standing.

"Which apartment?" he asked, pulling her backpack out of the backseat, where Mike, the helpful paramedic, had left it.

"Two-eleven," she answered, confirming his suspicions she was on the second floor. She swung her crutches forward and took a slow step forward. He stood right beside her, hating how her face went pale as she made her way slowly toward the apartment door.

He was sweating more than she was, just from watching her struggle. Ten times over he had to stop himself from just scooping her into his arms and carrying her in.

"Keys in the front pocket of my backpack," she said in a strained voice as she came to a halt in front of the main apartment door.

He found the keys, opened the lock and then held the door open for her. Thank God there was an elevator, so he wouldn't have to helplessly watch her attempt to maneuver the stairs.

When they reached her apartment door, he unlocked and opened it, holding it for her. She went inside, pausing in the tiny foyer.

"Thanks for the ride. I can take it from here," she said calmly, drumming up the most pathetic excuse for a smile.

Like hell she could. He ignored her, coming inside and closing the door firmly behind them. As he looked around at the inexpensive but neat furniture in the apartment, he asked, "How much food do you have?" Walking further into the room, he looped the strap of the backpack over the edge of a chair. How she managed to go grocery shopping on a bicycle was beyond him. "I'll run out and get you whatever you need."

Hailey eased herself onto the sofa with a low groan. He crossed over, helping her to lift her leg onto a pillow, elevating it. "I'm not sure," she said tiredly. "There's probably not much in the cupboards. I was planning to go shopping tomorrow.

She was clearly losing steam, not that he could blame her. He reached into her coat pocket and took out the pain pills. "You might need to take another one," he suggested, settling beside her on the sofa. "You can take two of them every four hours, as needed, and you only took one."

"Because it was a big horse pill," she muttered. But when he opened the bottle she held out her hand and took the tablet. He went to the kitchen, filled a glass with water and brought it back to her. She downed the second pain pill without hesitation.

He figured she'd be out like a light as soon as the second pill was absorbed into her system. And while she was sleeping, he'd take inventory to find out what she needed food-wise so he could shop for her.

But before that there was one question that had been burning in the back of his mind ever since the moment he'd tended to her at the side of the road. Maybe it wasn't completely fair to ask her now, when she was so clearly not herself, but he needed to know.

"Hailey?" When he sat beside her on the sofa, she opened her eyes and gazed up at him. Before he could talk himself out of it, he asked, "Who's Andrew?"

CHAPTER SIX

IN A heartbeat Hailey's exhaustion vanished. Every muscle in her body went tense, as she stared at Simon in stunned surprise.

How on earth had he known about Andrew?

Her flashback, she realized slowly. She must have said something to him during the moments at the side of the road when she'd been gripped in the horror of the past. She'd seen Andrew's face so clearly.

His pale, lifeless face. Streaked with blood.

Quickly she blocked the memory. No, don't go there. She needed to stay focused on the present.

But how to respond? Unfortunately, she couldn't bring herself to lie to Simon. Not after everything he'd done for her. Without his steadying presence, at the scene of the accident and in the emergency department, she knew the nightmares would have sucked her down into the whirling vortex of blackness that had characterized the last fourteen months.

She swallowed hard and tried to keep her voice from betraying her by trembling. "My fiancé."

Simon's eyes widened and she noticed he glanced at her ringless finger. "Why didn't you say something sooner?" he asked in a rush. "I didn't know you were engaged. We need to call Andrew to let him know you're all right."

She fought the urge to close her eyes and bury her face in the pillow, avoiding the painful subject. But she'd learned the hard way that hiding your head in the sand didn't make things go away. Simon wouldn't let her off the hook that easily. "No. I meant he was my fiancé. Andrew—he died a little over a year ago."

Fourteen months, to be exact. And she'd spent three of them recovering from the injuries she'd sustained in the accident in which he'd died.

But nothing would ever heal her heart. Or ease her conscience.

The usual sympathy darkened his eyes. "I'm sorry," he said simply.

Her stomach tightened painfully. She wanted to shout at him not to apologize. Why did everyone keep saying that? She was the reason Andrew was dead. She'd insisted on driving that night.

She didn't want Simon's sympathy.

Or anyone else's.

"I feel sick," she murmured, changing the subject as she put a hand over her abdomen. She wasn't lying, she really did feel sick. Throwing up would only make a bad day even worse, so she fought the urge and drew an uneven breath. "Would you mind bringing me a few saltine crackers?"

Instantly, he rose to his feet. "Of course not. Stay put, I'll find them."

"Third cabinet on the right," she murmured as Simon headed for the small kitchen. She took several shaky breaths. He rummaged around for a few minutes, and then returned with water and the promised crackers.

"You don't have any white soda," he said. "But don't worry, I'll run to the store and pick up a few things."

"There's no need," she began, but he cut her off.

"Don't argue. I'm going. It's not like you can live on jail fare," he said, gesturing to her water and crackers, "for the next few weeks."

"Rach can pick up some things for me," she pointed out stubbornly.

He didn't even look at her or acknowledge her statement. He simply stuck her door keys in his pocket and walked back to the kitchen. From her position on the sofa, she could hear him opening and closing the cupboard doors and her fridge, muttering to himself. Good thing she couldn't hear what he was saying, because it was no doubt something scathing, considering the bare state of her cabinets.

Old Mother Hubbard, went to the cupboard...

She wasn't destitute, but she did tend to buy sparingly because she had to lug everything on her bike. Or walk, which was actually much harder. At least on the bike she could cover the distance more quickly.

But she wasn't about to explain that to Simon.

After a good five minutes he returned, holding a list in his hand. A long list. "I'll be back in a little while. Take a nap," he suggested. "The best thing you can do right now is to rest."

Before she could think of a response, he left her apartment, softly shutting the door behind him.

She scowled at the closed door.

Sure. Take a nap. She grimaced as she tried to move

into a more comfortable position. Except she couldn't find a more comfortable position.

Wearily she closed her eyes and did her best to ignore the throbbing pain in her leg. Why hadn't she called Rachel for a ride to work that morning? What idiot rode a bike to work in a thunderstorm? Her ridiculous need to remain independent had cost her dearly.

Now she'd be dependent on others for help over the next who-knew-how-long. Two weeks for sure. Hopefully not longer. And as a new employee she didn't have any sick time to cover the time she'd need off work.

Maybe once she had a walking cast on, she could manage to ride her bike. At least well enough to get to work and home. If the hospital would let her work with her walking cast on.

With a sigh she decided not to worry about that now. First she needed to get through the next two weeks.

Surprisingly, she must have dozed because she awoke to a more intense throbbing in her leg. And the mouth-watering scent of chicken noodle soup.

Dusk had fallen. Her living room faced west, so it was easy to see through the window that the sun had set. She estimated the time must be somewhere close to seven o'clock.

She stretched, working the kinks out of her neck. Had Simon left some soup for her? She propped herself up on her elbow and leaned over to reach for her crutches standing upright against the edge of the end table nearby.

"Hailey, you're awake?" he asked, coming into the living room and startling her so badly she jerked like an epileptic and knocked the crutches to the floor with a crash.

"Cripes, don't do that!" she admonished, clutching a hand to her hammering heart. "You scared me to death."

"Sorry," Simon said with a grimace. "I didn't mean to startle you. I didn't think you were sleeping very soundly because you kept muttering in your sleep."

"I did?" She could feel her face flush. Talk about embarrassing. Although it could be worse. He could have told her she snored.

"Are you ready for more pain medication?" he asked. "It might be helpful to eat some soup first, so that your stomach doesn't get upset."

She wasn't sure which need took higher priority—her mouth watering and stomach growling for the soup or the throbbing in her leg.

"Soup," she finally decided, leaning over to pick up the fallen crutches from the floor. She narrowed her gaze when he swooped down to snatch the crutches before she could grab them. She sighed. "Look, Simon, I appreciate your help, but you don't need to stick around any longer. I'll be fine."

He stood holding the crutches, and lifted a sardonic brow. "Don't worry, I haven't exactly moved in yet," he said dryly, making her flush all over again. "Relax, all I did was pick up a few groceries and heat up some soup. Why don't you let me bring it in on a tray, so you don't have to get up?"

"Because soup would be easier to eat at the kitchen table. I'd prefer not to wear it." Somehow, she knew that once she got up and moving, she'd prove to Simon once and for all she was fine. And then he would leave.

At least, in theory.

Because surely that crack about moving in was a joke.

Wasn't it?

Yes, it was. She was losing her mind to think anything else. She gritted her teeth and swallowed a groan as she swung her leg over the edge of the sofa. Simon set the crutches aside and bent over to put his hands around her waist. Before she could squeak out a protest, he lifted her up on her good foot, supporting most of her weight.

She gripped his upper arms, momentarily distracted by the bulging muscles beneath her fingertips. His musky scent filled her head, making her dizzy.

Good heavens, she could stay here with him like this for the rest of the night without needing a single dose of pain medication.

"Let me know when you're ready," he murmured, his mouth dangerously close to her ear.

Ready? For what? To fall into his arms? To be swept down the hall to her bedroom?

"I'm—uh—ready," she said breathlessly, forcing herself to concentrate. She needed to move away. And fast. "You can—uh—hand me the crutches now."

For what seemed like endless moments neither one of them moved. She held her breath, waiting for what she had no idea, but every nerve in her body was tingling in awareness. The throbbing pain in her leg was nothing compared to the blood rushing through her system.

But then Simon moved one of the hands at her waist

to bring over the crutches. He tucked one beneath her arm, and she reluctantly let go of his biceps to grasp the crutch. Then he handed her the second crutch.

When he was sure she was steady on her feet, he backed away. She kept her gaze on trained on the floor as she cautiously swung the crutches forward, moving slowly toward the kitchen.

There was an empty bowl on the table sitting beside the small bottle of pain medication and a fresh package of crackers. As she lowered herself into the chair, Simon filled her bowl from the steaming pot on the stove and set it back down in front of her.

"Do you need anything else?" he asked, when she took a sip of the soup.

She nearly scalded her tongue. "No, Simon, this is perfect. Just what I needed. Thanks. For driving me home, shopping and cooking for me."

A ghost of a smile flirted with his lips. "You're welcome."

As much as she wanted him to leave, for her peace of mind more than anything, she gestured to the empty seat at the table beside her. "Please, join me. I'm sure you're hungry, too."

He moved as if to do just that, but then stopped abruptly. "Ah, no, thanks. I should probably get going. Are you sure you'll be okay here alone? I could wait until you've finished eating if you think you need help getting settled for the night."

This time she did scald her tongue and she took a sip of white soda to cool the burning. The thought of Simon anywhere near her bedroom made her break out into a cold sweat.

Not because she didn't want him there.

Just the opposite.

"I'm sure I'll be fine," she said firmly, tearing her thoughts from that traitorous path. She was not going to wonder what it would be like to kiss Simon.

Not. Going. There.

"I'm not helpless, you know," she said tartly. "I'm not the first person with a broken leg and I won't be the last."

She caught a glimpse of his grim expression before it vanished. "Okay, then. Here's my cell phone number." He slid a slip of paper across the table toward her with his number scrawled on it in his bold script. "I want you to promise me you'll call if you need anything."

"All right," she agreed, knowing she wouldn't. If she'd call anyone it would be Rachel. Not Simon.

No matter how tempting.

"Thanks again, Simon." She took another sip of her soup, hoping he'd take the hint.

He did. "Goodnight, Hailey." He stared at her for several long seconds before turning on his heel and walking toward the door.

She held her breath until he shut the apartment door quietly behind him.

Letting out a ragged sigh, she dropped her spoon and buried her face in her hands.

And fought the overwhelming urge to call him back.

Simon left Hailey's apartment, calling himself every kind of fool.

Hailey would be fine. He was being a total idiot for overreacting like this. She would be absolutely fine.

A broken leg wasn't the end of the world. Logically, he knew that.

But he couldn't help feeling responsible. It was his fault she was laid up for the next two weeks at least.

He didn't need to keep checking on her. Unless she called. Which he knew she wouldn't.

Hailey was perfectly able to take care of herself.

Shoving his hands in his pockets, he ducked his head against the drizzle and walked out to his car. As he headed home, the thought of sitting around in his empty house made him restless. Normally he yearned for some quiet time. He'd just bought a new book but tonight the idea of losing himself in a great story did not hold any appeal. In fact, he didn't want to go home.

He'd wanted to stay with Hailey.

Not an option, he reminded himself harshly. Then what? Call Jadon? Or Quinn? Nah, both men had families of their own.

Executing a safe and legal U-turn, he turned the car around to head back toward Cedar Bluff hospital.

"What are you doing here?" Seth asked, seemingly exasperated when he strolled in. "Hell, Simon, I'm here covering you so you can have the night off."

"I know, but things have changed." Simon forced a smile. "I'm here to finish my shift, so you can go back home to your pretty pregnant wife and son."

"I don't think so," Seth argued lightly. "For one thing, you don't look as if you've really recovered from hitting Hailey. Not that I blame you, that had to be horrible. But honestly? I could really use the money as I missed that shift the other day. Kylie really wants to move into a newer and bigger house before the baby is born. We're scraping up some money for a decent down payment."

Damn. The one argument he couldn't fight. He'd never take a needed shift away from a colleague, much less a friend.

Seth could finish off the shift if he wanted to.

But Simon still didn't want to go home to his empty house. He glanced around, almost desperate for something to keep his mind occupied. With a frown, he noticed the census board wasn't overly filled with patients. "I could still help out—if things are crazy. Free of charge," he added hoping he didn't sound as pathetic as he felt.

"Nope," Seth said cheerfully. "No worries, we have everything under control. Seriously, man, it's just not that busy."

It figured. Monday nights were generally one of the quietest days of the week.

"How's Hailey?" Seth asked with a keen glance.

Simon wasn't fooled by his friend's deceptively casual tone. The last thing he or Hailey needed was for rumors to start flying. And considering how he'd held her hand during her examination in the trauma bay, he figured the rumors were already brewing. "Fine, considering I slammed into her with my car and nearly killed her."

Seth arched a brow. "I don't think a broken leg qualifies as nearly killing her. But, hey, glad to hear she's doing all right."

"Yeah, well, she made it pretty clear she wanted me gone, so I don't think she shares your view of the accident," Simon countered.

But Seth only grinned. "And that's bugging the hell out of you, isn't it?"

Simon was about to tell him to shut the hell up when he saw, out of the corner of his eye, that the new unit clerk, Mary something or other, was blatantly eavesdropping on their conversation. Her eyes, dramatically green from colored contacts, shifted under his gaze and she turned away.

He grimaced. Great. More fuel for the gossip mill. He loved living in Cedar Bluff, but compared to the blissful anonymity he'd experienced in Chicago, living in this place was like living in a bubble where everyone stuck their noses into everyone else's business.

Which normally wasn't a problem for him. People in Cedar Bluff usually left him alone, because obviously he'd never given them anything to talk about.

Until now.

"Hardly," he said, narrowing his gaze on Seth, silently warning him to drop it. "And if you don't need my help, fine. I have some paperwork to finish in my office, anyway. There are several quality cases that need to be reviewed."

"You're hopeless, my friend. Truly hopeless," Seth muttered, shaking his head in mock dismay. "What a lame way to spend your night off."

Simon ignored him. Seth couldn't know that tossing and turning in his bed, thinking of Hailey, would be far worse than any torture imaginable. "If you get slammed with patients, let me know."

"Sure," Seth said, glancing down as his trauma pager began to vibrate. "No worries."

Simon did his best to concentrate on the cases he

needed to review, but after reading the same case three times without comprehension he shoved it away with a disgusted sigh.

Seth was right. He was truly hopeless.

He shut off his computer and stood. When he dug in his pocket for his car keys, he realized he still had Hailey's apartment keys.

For a long agonizing moment he wondered if he'd subconsciously kept them on purpose.

Because now he had a good excuse to see Hailey again.

CHAPTER SEVEN

THE next morning Hailey crutch-walked the short distance from her bed to the bathroom, groaning under her breath with each clunky step.

Every muscle in her body was sore. Muscles she hadn't known she possessed hurt. But the good news was that her leg didn't throb as badly as it had yesterday.

From here on, she'd probably start feeling better each day.

It took her much longer than normal to get showered and dressed, especially as her cast had to be wrapped with plastic for the shower, and then afterward the bulky covering didn't fit into the pants leg of her jeans. She had to rip out the side seam out of an old pair of sweats, topped with an equally ragged T-shirt, so she wouldn't have to walk around in her underwear.

She ate a bowl of cereal for breakfast and then cradled a mug of coffee in her hands, the day looming endlessly before her. Often she'd wished for a few days off to get caught up on errands and such, but not like this. Not wearing a cast that prevented her from doing anything.

The scrap of paper with Simon's number was still sitting on the kitchen table, mocking her. Last night she'd actually tossed the note into the garbage, but had then changed her mind and dug it back out again, smoothing out the crumpled edges.

Stupid, because she didn't plan on calling him.

But it had been sweet of him to leave it for her. In fact, Simon had been wonderful, in many ways.

She gave herself a mental shake. There was no point reading anything but basic kindness in his motives for helping her. She knew that even though she'd taken the blame for what had happened, he still felt responsible.

Simon was honorable that way. And maybe a bit stubborn.

Just because she found him devastatingly attractive, it didn't mean he felt even remotely the same way about her.

And even if he did, they were colleagues. Maybe even friends. Nothing more.

Anxious for something to do, she headed for her bedroom and the looming pile of laundry waiting for her there. Of course, if she'd known she was going to break her leg, she would have made sure her laundry was caught up.

Where was that crystal ball when you needed it?

She had to leave her mug of coffee on the kitchen table as she couldn't crutch-walk and carry it at the same time. Neither could she carry her laundry basket.

Muttering a naughty word under her breath, she used her crutches to shove the laundry basket piled high with dirty clothes across the carpeting and down the hall, until she reached the kitchen.

Doing the laundry would take her twice as long on crutches, but it wasn't like she had other burning plans anyway. Watching television was sure to get boring. Maybe Rachel would stop at the local video store to pick her up some movies to watch.

While seated on the kitchen chair, she split her laundry into two loads, and then went back to the hallway closet to get the bottle of laundry soap, dangling it from her two fingers while manipulating the crutches. Thank heavens her apartment was small.

Crutches were really a pain in the butt.

Once she had the clothes divided and a load in the laundry basket, she looked around for her keys.

Of course, she couldn't find them.

After ten minutes of looking, she gave up. The last time she'd seen them had been when Simon had taken them to go grocery shopping.

Had he inadvertently taken them with him last night?

Possibly. Maybe she should call him. Her heart leaped at the idea. But she just as quickly shut it down.

Pathetic. She was truly pathetic.

The building manager had a spare key. She could just as easily get it from him. She had, in fact, done that very thing the last time she'd accidentally locked her keys inside the apartment while doing laundry.

There was no need to bother Simon.

But she needed to prop the door open somehow, so she jammed a pair of dirty scrubs beneath the apartment door to keep it from closing. From there, she pushed the laundry basket full of clothes down the hall in front of her until she reached the elevator.

Once she had the load into the washer, she was able to grab the empty laundry basket with the edge of her fingers and carry it back up to her apartment. She made better time, although the empty basket was bulky and kept bouncing against the wall along the way.

When she reached her apartment, though, the tip of her crutch got tangled up in the scrubs she'd jammed beneath the door. For a moment she teetered precariously as she tried to regain her balance while untangling the tip of the crutch, but then she toppled over. And hit the floor.

Hard.

More bruises, she thought with a weary wince as she tried to catch her breath.

"Hailey? My God, are you all right?"

Sprawled inelegantly on the floor just inside her apartment, with the empty laundry basket on lying on top of her, she glanced up to find Simon standing in the doorway. He looked incredible in a long-sleeved denim shirt and well-worn blue jeans. She shoved her hair out of her eyes.

Seriously, the man had the absolute worst timing.

Simon scowled as he tossed the empty laundry basket aside and looked Hailey over, assessing the damage. He saw the scrubs stuffed under the door and figured they'd gotten tangled in her crutches, causing the fall. His fault for taking the stupid keys in the first place. He should have dropped them off late last night before she'd gone to sleep. "Are you sure you didn't hurt yourself?"

"Only my pride," she muttered, pushing herself upright.

"Here, grab my hands and then bend your good leg," he instructed. "I'll help lift you up."

"I swear I'm not usually this clumsy," she said, as he hauled her upright with a smooth motion. Once she was standing on her good foot, he put his arm around her waist to steady her.

"I know," he said reassuringly.

"You seem to have a knack for seeing me at my worst," she grumbled, as he helped her over to the kitchen chair.

"Hailey, you look fine. I'm glad I was here to help."

Once he had her safely seated, he pulled the scrubs out from beneath the door and then closed it. He picked up the rest of the clothes scattered across the floor, tossing the items into the empty basket.

"Please, just leave them. I'll pick them up," she protested.

He ignored her, finishing the task while taking care not to examine the frilly, lacy items too closely. He pushed the basket out of the way and glanced at her. "I guess you realize I accidentally took your keys," he murmured, pulling out a chair to sit next to her. He was somewhat surprised to see his phone number still sitting on the kitchen table. "Why didn't you call me? I would have brought back your keys and hauled your stuff down to the laundry room, too."

She avoided his direct gaze. "I needed the door to stay open anyway, because it's too hard to maneuver it along with the crutches. And the keys were no big deal. I would have borrowed a spare set from the manager."

"I see." He stared at her, trying to figure out why she seemed to be going out of her way to avoid him. He blew out a heavy breath. "Hailey, I'm sorry about hitting you and causing all this. I feel awful. I wish there was something I could do to make it up to you."

"Simon, you have to stop acting like I'm badly injured," she said, clearly exasperated. "You've already helped me a lot. More than anyone else would have done. You wouldn't even let me pay you for the groceries."

No, he wouldn't. And now that he was here, he didn't plan on leaving anytime soon. She was obviously too stubborn for her own good. She was lucky she hadn't hurt herself worse with that earlier stunt.

Why on earth she'd had the burning need to do laundry first thing this morning was beyond him. No lounging around and resting for Hailey. He reached over to lightly grasp her hand. "I'm not working today, so my entire day is free. Just tell me what you need. I'm all yours."

Her head jerked up, her surprised gaze colliding with his. A sizzling awareness shimmered in the air between them. For long seconds neither one of them said anything. Belatedly, he realized how his last words might have sounded.

I'm all yours.

For the first time since Erica, he wished they were true. After the constant emotional drama, and the subsequent loss, he'd been more than content to live his life alone, without the entanglement of a relationship.

Yet looking down into Hailey's bright blue eyes, he understood what he'd been missing. Until now, he hadn't realized the restlessness he thought he'd been feeling might actually be pure loneliness.

When the silence stretched to the point where it became downright uncomfortable, he let go of her hand

and cleared his throat. "So what are your plans for the day? Aside from laundry," he added, glancing at the basket. "I'd be happy to finish up the loads for you, but that won't take long."

"No plans, really," she said with a careless shrug. "What can I do? I don't have a lot of money, especially now that I can't work for the next two weeks. I was actually thinking of calling Theresa to see if there was any way I could do something to get a few hours in. But other than that, I'm pretty much stuck here. There isn't a whole lot of things to do within walking distance."

He made a mental note to approach Theresa himself to plead Hailey's case. Surely there were some chart audits for their upcoming joint commission survey she could do. And he could actually use her help with the quality-of-care cases that he'd only just begun to review.

"Okay, then, let me ask you this," he said. "What would you do today if you could get out of here for a while?"

"Go to the park," she answered, seemingly without thinking. "Maybe stop at the library or the video store to rent a few movies. But you certainly don't have to be my babysitter, Simon. I plan to give Rachel a call later. I'm not totally helpless, you know."

He stared at her for a moment. He didn't want her to call Rachel. Or anyone else for that matter. "Hailey, I never once thought you were helpless. Quite the opposite."

Her smile seemed a bit sad. "Well, thanks for stopping by to return the keys. I'm sure you have better things to do with your day off."

He understood that she'd continue to shove him away unless he made her understand how he really felt. Opening himself up wasn't easy. But neither was walking away. "What if I told you I didn't want to spend the day alone?" he asked softly. "What if I told you I'd much rather spend time with you?"

There was another pause, and he almost wished he'd kept his big mouth shut.

But she smiled. "I'd say I'm glad to hear that, because I'd like to spend the day with you, too."

He grinned, a feeling of relief sweeping over him rather than the usual sense of dread that normally curled in his gut whenever he'd considered seeing a woman on a personal level.

Hailey was different. Or rather his feelings toward her were different. And right now he couldn't find the energy to care if he was walking along the edge of a slippery slope as long as Hailey was beside him.

Hailey watched Simon haul her laundry bag of dirty clothes out of the apartment, wondering if she had rocks for brains.

Why had she agreed to let him help? Especially with something as personal as her laundry? Just the thought of him looking at her intimate wear made her blush.

But even worse, why had she agreed to spend the entire day with him?

She wanted to think he'd simply caught her in a weak moment but, in truth, she'd agreed because she wanted to spend the day with him.

Treading into dangerous territory? Maybe. But she shoved her misgivings aside. For too long her response to men had been non-existent, and now that her emotions had thawed, she found she liked having them. And the thought of being cooped up inside the tiny apartment wasn't at all appealing, so why not take advantage of Simon's generosity?

He didn't have to know how much she admired him. She'd treat him like a friend. Surely everyone could use a few friends?

Thankfully, Simon didn't insist on doing everything. He brought the clean clothes up from the basement laundry room and gave her the opportunity to fold the items and put them away.

He was on the phone when she emerged from the bedroom. He quickly finished his call and snapped the cell phone shut when he saw her.

"I'm sorry, but I don't have much to wear other than this," she said, gesturing to the slit-up-the-side-seam sweat pants.

"That's okay," he said, waving away her concern. "We're only going to the park, to the library and to the video store."

She rolled her eyes. "I don't think we have to cover everything I mentioned."

He simply cocked a brow. "Well, as the sun is shining and it's a balmy sixty degrees outside, why don't we go to the park first? If you're up to it we can make another stop or two at the library or the video store on the way home."

"Sounds good." She went over to her purse to pull out her sunglasses. She followed Simon down the hall, going through the doors he held open for her.

"I can't believe how nice it is outside after the storm yesterday," she said, squinting in the glare of the sun.

"I know. Good thing the storm didn't do any major damage." Simon held the passenger door open for her.

She hesitated just for a moment. Riding in a car as a passenger wasn't her favorite pastime, but she'd managed to get over her fear to a certain extent. And she didn't have much of a choice now that she'd broken her leg. This would be the beginning of many car rides.

She could do this. No problem.

Taking a deep breath, she slid into the passenger seat, extremely conscious of Simon's hand under her elbow. His touch, even as light and impersonal as it was, helped distract her from being in the car.

She could get used to having his hands on her.

Giving a mental eye roll, she stared forward through the windshield, determined not to let her idiotic fantasies ruin the day.

When they arrived at Cedar Bluff park, there were two paths, one that climbed up to the top of the bluff and one that lead down to the lakefront. If not for the crutches she would have preferred to go up, but when Simon started out along the path leading down to the lake, she fell into step beside him.

The sun was warm on her skin, and the light breeze coming off the lake felt refreshingly wonderful. She loved the rhythmic sounds of the waves crashing over the rocky shore.

"I'm so glad we came," she said, pausing for a moment to tuck her hair behind her ears to keep it out of her eyes. "I didn't realize how much I needed to get out of that stuffy apartment."

"I'm glad we came too," Simon murmured. He walked slowly alongside her, keeping pace with her awkward gait, his hand resting lightly on the small of her back.

She imagined that anyone watching them would think they were a couple. The thought caused a tingle of awareness. She glanced around, thinking it was a good thing the lakefront was deserted on a Tuesday in the middle of the day.

"Hailey, do you mind if I ask you a question?"

She glanced at him in surprise. "Of course not."

"The day we took care of that young seventeen-year-old motor vehicle crash victim, you seemed to take his death pretty hard. Was that because he reminded you of your fiancé, Andrew?"

They'd reached the lakeshore so she stopped, staring out at the rippling water for a moment. "Yes."

"Because he died in a car crash too?" Simon asked persistently.

"Yes." She turned toward Simon, suddenly tempted to tell him the truth. All of the truth.

Even the parts she'd never told anyone.

But the words stuck in her throat.

"Is that why you don't drive a car?" he asked. "I mean, I had this brilliant idea to offer to share my car with you, but even if I did, you wouldn't drive it, would you?"

Obviously, he had all the answers, so why bother with the questions? She blew out a breath, amazed that he'd nailed the truth. She'd already told him about Andrew so it wasn't much of a stretch to put two and two together and come up with four. "No, I wouldn't," she finally admitted. "But thanks for the kind offer."

"Why not? You seemed fine riding as a passenger. Why not drive a car?"

"I can't," she said helplessly, avoiding his gaze. "I don't enjoy riding in a car as a passenger, either. But the reason I go everywhere on my bike is because I haven't driven a car since the accident. Because I was driving that night. The crash—Andrew's death—was my fault."

"Hailey," he murmured, and suddenly he took one of her crutches out of the way so he could pull her into his arms. His musky scent intermingled with the fresh air coming off the lake. "No, don't say that. Sometimes things happen. Like you and me colliding in the rain. Didn't you tell me that hitting you wasn't my fault? It's the same thing."

No, it wasn't. He didn't know the whole story. How she'd insisted on driving that night because Andrew had had a few drinks. They'd argued, heatedly. And in the end her decision had cost him his life. If she'd let him drive, she would have been in the passenger seat.

She didn't want to relive the painful memories. She could feel Simon's intent gaze. It was tempting, so tempting to hide her face in the hollow of his shoulder. To simply give herself over to his warm embrace.

Gathering her courage, she forced herself to meet his compassionate chocolate-brown gaze.

But before she could say anything to make him understand, she was distracted by his mouth, dangerously close to hers. And whatever thought she was about to voice flew right out of her head.

She must have been a little too obvious because he murmured her name again, almost like a plea, before his mouth came down to capture hers.

CHAPTER EIGHT

THE urgency of Hailey's response, the way her lips parted invitingly, made it impossible for Simon to pull away. Instead, he broke every one of his rules by deepening the kiss.

He wanted her. More than he could ever remember wanting anyone else. Her taste was like a drug and he was willing to suffer any consequences in order to have more. In some distant part of his mind he remembered to be careful of her broken leg, although he crushed her close, enjoying the way her soft curves pressed against him.

She fitted in his arms perfectly.

Reluctantly, he broke off the kiss when he heard a dog walker approaching. They were standing right in the middle of the narrow path so they needed to get out of the way. He steadied Hailey with one hand and bent over to pick up her discarded crutches from the ground.

Hailey gripped his arm like it was a lifeline, balancing her weight on her good leg. The dazed expression in her eyes only made him want to kiss her again.

How would she look if they made love?

His pulse skyrocketed at the mere thought. He pulled

himself together with an effort, ignoring his body's physical response. Even this kiss shouldn't have happened.

He couldn't take things between them any further. Giving in to his libido had cost him more than he could bear with Erica.

"Sorry about that," Simon murmured, tucking each of her crutches beneath her arms.

She grasped the handles of the crutches and moved out of the walker's way. She looked up at him, her expression uncertain. "I'm not sure I understand what you're apologising for," she said.

He swallowed a curse. This wasn't Hailey's fault. It was his. He didn't know what in the hell he'd been thinking to kiss her like that. And no matter how much he wanted to avoid the topic, Hailey deserved the truth. "I—uh—shouldn't have kissed you."

Her gaze dropped to the ground. "I see." Without saying anything more, she pivoted and continued walking down the path toward the lakefront.

Dammit. Now he'd made her feel bad. He quickened his pace to catch up to her. "Hailey, I'm sorry."

"Yeah. You already said that." Her clipped tone and hurried pace were the only outward signs of her anger.

"Let me explain, please?" She was crutch-walking at a fast pace and he had to lengthen his stride to keep up with her. "It's not that I didn't want to kiss you—" he began.

"Don't." Her sharp tone interrupted him. "Don't bother giving me the *it's not you, it's me* speech, okay?

I get it. I already heard from Rachel how you have a rule about not dating women you work with."

He couldn't completely hide his surprise. "She told you?"

She flashed him a disgusted look. "Yes, she told me. And, really, it's no big deal. We'll just forget that this—uh—interlude ever happened." She grimaced and kept her gaze purposely away from his.

Forget about their kiss? Not bloody likely.

Although maybe she wasn't as affected by what had happened as he was. The thought was sobering.

He sighed, and found himself wanting to explain. He'd never told anyone about Erica. He'd been too embarrassed to admit how far over the top she'd gone.

And the role he'd played in the fallout. The memory still tortured him.

No, he couldn't tell her everything. Not his deepest, darkest secret. But he had to tell her something.

"It's not a bad rule," he muttered defensively. "If you date people you work with and then something doesn't work out, it's a mess. Everyone ends up affected, not just the people who were in the relationship."

She stopped so abruptly he almost knocked into her. She swung around to pierce him with her direct gaze. "Is that what happened to you?"

The fiasco with Erica was so much more than that, but it was easier just to nod. "Yeah. And it was bad. So I made up my mind not to repeat that mistake ever again."

She continued to stare at him for several long seconds. "You're right," she agreed softly. "It's not a bad rule."

His mouth dropped open in surprise, and disappointment stabbed deep. For a ridiculous moment he wanted her to argue with him, to reassure him that things between them could work out. That even if their relationship didn't last, they'd always be professional enough to work together without dragging their personal lives into the mix.

What a load of rubbish. He really had it bad to even attempt to rationalize this.

Hailey resumed walking and he followed more slowly, scrubbing his hand over his face, knowing he should be glad she wasn't making this difficult for him.

Yet irrationally annoyed that she could drop what had just transpired between them so easily.

When they reached the lakefront, Hailey stopped and gazed silently out at the rhythmically rolling waves. For several long moments neither of them said anything.

"Thanks for bringing me out here, Simon," she finally said. When she turned to face him, her earlier irritation seemed to have vanished. "I…really hope we can remain friends."

Friends? Was she kidding? The urge to sweep her into his arms again, to kiss her senseless, was overwhelming. Every cell in his body protested the idea of simply being friends.

But he forced himself to nod. "Of course, Hailey. I value you as a friend."

Relief flooded her gaze. "I'm glad. Now that we have that settled, do you mind if I sit on one of these rocks to rest a minute? I'm exhausted."

Without waiting for a response, she made her way over to a large, flat rock.

And despite knowing she was right, he couldn't ignore the devastating sense that he'd just lost something precious.

Hailey kept up the pretense of being Simon's friend throughout the events of the day—the trip to the library, where she discovered they had identical taste in fiction, to the video store, where she discovered they had completely opposite tastes in movies, and throughout the impromptu dinner at a small Italian restaurant that seemed a little too cozy and romantic to be just a dinner for two friends.

Not until Simon had dropped her off at home did she collapse onto the sofa and close her eyes in despair.

There was no way in the world she could do this again. Pretending to be just friends with Simon was too difficult.

And painful.

Despite her exhaustion, images of their day together continued to flash in her mind, like a slide show. Simon intensely discussing the latest novel he was reading. His grimace when she'd picked out a couple of romantic comedies from the video store. The blatant desire in his eyes after he'd kissed her.

She did her best to block them out, especially that last image, but when she opened her eyes and stared up at the ceiling she felt like crying.

Maybe she didn't deserve happiness. After Andrew's death she'd truly believed she'd suffer for ever. She had punished herself for what she believed had been her fault.

But then she had learned that life really did move on. And the bouts of self-pity came less and less frequently. She'd even found herself laughing on occasion.

For a few minutes there on the path, when Simon had kissed her, she'd begun to believe she might be ready for another relationship.

Only to have that hope brutally squashed.

Okay, enough self-pity, she told herself sternly. One kiss did not a relationship make.

The fact that she'd responded to Simon at all was good news. If she was attracted to Simon, surely she could be attracted to someone else?

Of course she could.

The role she'd played in Andrew's death had changed her. But maybe she'd been changed for the better?

Taking a deep breath, she pulled herself upright, groaning under her breath as her aching muscles protested painfully.

No matter how sore she was from being out all day, she refused to regret one moment. At least in Simon's arms she'd felt truly alive.

The next two days were excruciatingly long and boring for Hailey. Despite the books she'd picked up at the library and the movies she'd watched with Rachel, the two days seemed like a lifetime.

How she'd get through two full weeks, she wasn't sure.

On the third day her cell phone rang and her heart

irrationally leaped in her chest as she grabbed the phone, peering at the screen.

Her hope deflated. Not Simon.

Her boss. She forced a cheerfulness she didn't feel into her tone. "Hi, Theresa. Did you get my leave-of-absence paperwork?"

"Ah, yes, I did." Theresa cleared her throat on the other end of the line. "But, Hailey, I'm afraid I have some bad news. I don't think your leave of absence will be approved because you've only been working here two months. Normally, you have to be working for a full twelve months in order to get approved for a leave of absence."

She sank into her kitchen chair, her crutches dropping to the floor with a crash. It took a few minutes to find her voice. "What does that mean?"

"I don't know for sure," Theresa admitted. "I'm waiting to hear back from Human Resources. The good news is that your health insurance will cover the costs of your treatment for the accident. But normally we have a return-to-work program for staff on medical leave so they can do light-duty functions, and I'm afraid you won't qualify."

"Does that mean I have to leave?" Ironically, the first thought that entered her mind was that if she was forced to quit her job, she wouldn't be Simon's coworker any more. His rule wouldn't apply.

But on the heels of that, practical logic kicked in. When the full realization hit, her stomach sank.

"No, you don't have to quit. But you won't get any payment for being off work either."

No payments. And no way to return to work for the

full time her leg was in a cast? "Theresa, please, isn't there some way I can qualify for returning to work on light duty? I need to be able to pay my rent. I'd be willing to do anything—paperwork, or even a triage nurse..."

"No, not as a triage nurse," Theresa said firmly. "Hailey, you can't be on crutches and take care of patients. If a patient's condition suddenly deteriorated, you'd need to be able to respond immediately. And if you hurt yourself in the process, we'd be responsible from a worker's compensation perspective."

She couldn't argue against her boss's logic. "Okay, paperwork, then. I can't be hurt doing paperwork. I could do chart reviews. The schedule. I'll be your assistant. I'll function as a unit clerk. Anything you want me to do." She halted, realizing she was close to begging.

"I'll see what I can work out with Human Resources," Theresa hedged. "We have work you can do, but the problem is that you don't qualify for the program because you haven't been here long enough."

Hailey swallowed hard. "Is there anything I can do to help plead my case?"

"I'll see what I can do," Theresa promised. "Maybe if I explain how we badly we need some chart audits done before our joint commission visit, they'll give in."

Hope flared. "I can do chart audits," she quickly interjected. "You tell me when and where. I'll do a hundred chart audits."

"I need to get approval from the vice president of Human Resources first," Theresa cautioned. "But I'll ask and let you know, okay?"

"Today?" She grimaced at her pathetically hopeful tone.

"Soon," Theresa promised. "Give me a day or two, all right?"

"All right. Thanks, Theresa." Hailey snapped her phone shut and tried to quell her rising panic.

Surely they'd let her do something. Wouldn't they?

She buried her face in her hands and battled the irrational urge to call Simon. She hadn't seen or spoken to him since the day of their kiss. The day she'd pretended to feel nothing but friendship toward him.

No, she couldn't call him.

She tried Rachel, and ended up leaving a message. Maybe she could help sway Theresa, as Rachel had worked here in Cedar Bluff for a few years.

Of course, Simon might be willing to put a good word in for her, too.

Maybe.

She tried to lose herself in a book, but after reading the same few pages several times she gave up.

Instead, she decided to balance her checkbook. She had a banking program on her computer, so she turned on her laptop and went meticulously through her financial situation.

The news was grim. She would only be able to hold onto her apartment for another six weeks without a paycheck and the rent was due in two weeks.

This time, when her cell phone rang, she held her breath and closed her eyes as she answered it, hoping Theresa wasn't calling with bad news.

"Hi, Hailey, how are you?" The deep voice was Simon's. She was so surprised she didn't answer immediately.

"I'm okay." She mentally winced at her lackluster

response. She tried to brighten her tone. "How are you? Busy at work?"

"What's wrong?" Simon asked. "You sound upset."

So much for her attempt to sound cheerful. Since she was feeling desperate, she put her pride aside. "I am upset. Apparently the hospital won't approve my leave of absence because I haven't worked there for a full year. My boss told me I don't qualify for the return to work light-duty program."

"What? That's ridiculous." Simon's outrage on her behalf made her smile. "So what if you haven't been here a year? There are plenty of things to do. In fact, I need help with some quality reviews. I'm going to talk to Theresa."

"Really?" She couldn't hide her flash of excitement. "Oh, Simon, it would be great if I could help out. Even part-time hours. Anything."

"I'll call you right back."

Simon didn't call right back, and in the hour that passed she convinced herself he'd been unable to plead her case. A good hour later, Theresa called.

"Hailey? I managed to convince Human Resources to cut you a break and bend our policy. You're approved for light-duty work but only part-time hours. You'll do chart audits for us and quality review cases for Simon Carter. Do you think you can start with a few hours this afternoon?"

"Yes!" she exclaimed. "Absolutely! Thank you, Theresa. You don't know how much this means to me."

"All right, be here about one o'clock and we'll go over what needs to be done."

Hailey had been so excited about working she'd forgotten she didn't have a bike. "I'll be there," she rashly promised.

She'd crutch-walk the three miles if she had to.

But, of course, Simon called her back almost immediately after her conversation with Theresa. "Hailey? I'll be there at twelve-thirty to pick you up."

"I'll be ready," she assured him. "And, Simon? Thanks for going to bat for me."

"Anytime," he said gruffly.

Wearing scrubs, the wide pants legs just barely fitting over her cast, she couldn't hide her relief as she and Simon walked into the busy emergency department. Because Theresa was busy trying to fill a sick call, Simon took her into his office.

"Here's a list of cases I'd like you to review." He handed her a slip of paper with ten patient names on it. "Go through the computer records and let me know if you think the medical staff and nursing staff provided appropriate care."

"All right," she agreed. "Is there a reason to believe the care wasn't appropriate?"

He hesitated. "I'd rather not answer that until you've reviewed them with fresh eyes."

She could see his point. If she knew his opinion, she'd likely look at each patient's record differently. He was asking for a nonjudgmental approach. "Where would you like me to work?"

"You'll have to find a workstation out at the main desk by the unit clerk," he said, glancing toward the arena just a stone's throw from his office. "I have some things I need to do in here."

"Okay." She ignored the flash of disappointment that they wouldn't be working more closely together. What did it matter where she worked? She was truly grateful for the paperwork assignment that would help pay her rent.

She sat down at the only empty computer, not far from the unit clerk. There was so much activity, though, that she quickly became distracted by the orders that came flying toward the poor woman. Orders for labs, X-rays, consultants—it seemed like the list was never ending.

"Would you like some help?" she asked Mary, the unit clerk on duty. The woman was close to her own age, but looked older because of her bleached blonde hair, which was cut short and was spiky with gel. Her green eyes were too bright to be real, so they had to be from colored contact lenses. She'd tried to befriend the woman, as Mary was also relatively new to Cedar Bluff.

"No." The rude response took her by surprise, especially when the woman pretty much ignored her. "I don't need your help."

Okay, then. With a shrug, Hailey turned her attention back to the task at hand. She made a Herculean effort to block out all the noise around her, concentrating on the notes in the patient's chart.

Her elbow was roughly jostled by someone next to her and she looked up in time to see the tech, Bonnie, trying to reach around her, holding a full glass of water. One moment the cup was in Bonnie's hand, the next it had been dumped into her lap, soaking her scrubs and the computer monitor.

Hailey leaped up from her seat, trying to shake off the water pooling in her lap, but forgot about her cast until pain shot up her leg as she put her full weight on it. She fell against the edge of the desk with a cry.

Pain reverberated down her hip to her leg, her scrub pants were soaked and the computer screen had gone completely blank.

"I'm so sorry!" Bonnie exclaimed in horror.

CHAPTER NINE

SIMON overheard a ruckus out at the main desk in the arena, and as he couldn't concentrate, thanks to distracting memories of kissing Hailey, he came out to investigate.

Hailey was leaning heavily against the edge of the desk without her crutches, her expression a pained grimace as she tried to shoo several well-meaning staff members away. The dampness of her scrubs and the upended cup of water lying on the computer keyboard bore testament as to what had happened.

"I'm fine," she insisted, using the paper towels someone had brought over to mop up the mess. "But we need to call a tech from IT to fix the computer."

He came over at the same time Theresa approached from the opposite direction, her brows pulled together in a deep frown. "Hailey? You don't look very good. Are you sure you didn't injure yourself?"

Hailey's smile was strained and he suspected the pain was far worse than she was letting on. "I didn't hurt myself, Theresa, but unfortunately the water took out the computer monitor."

For a long moment Hailey and Theresa stared at each

other, until Theresa finally glanced away. "Maybe this wasn't such a good idea."

Hailey paled, her blue eyes standing out starkly against the rest of her features. Simon had the uncharacteristic urge to reassure her that everything would be okay.

"Theresa, please," she said a bit desperately. "I swear this wasn't my fault. It was an unfortunate accident with a bit of spilled water, nothing more."

Simon readily jumped to Hailey's defense. "I'm the one who told Hailey to come out to the front desk to work. I should have let her use my office."

Theresa looked torn. He understood. As the nurse manager for the area, she shouldered a heavy responsibility. "I don't know, if Hailey hurts herself while working here…" She didn't finish the thought but he knew exactly what she meant. He'd learned all about worker's compensation laws when one of the residents had been injured on duty.

Theresa didn't want the hospital to be legally responsible for adding to Hailey's injury. He could respect that.

"She won't hurt herself doing chart reviews," he said firmly. "I'll get the computer fixed and from now on Hailey can sit in my office to complete the reviews." He was determined to make this work out, so Hailey would have some sort of income, as it was primarily his fault that she was unable to perform her normal duties as an ED nurse.

He'd find something to occupy his time elsewhere. Heaven knew, his office was not big enough for the both of them.

Another long silence hung in the air, before Theresa finally nodded. "All right. I guess she can do the chart reviews in your office."

"Thank you, Theresa," Hailey murmured, her relief and gratitude evident. "I promise you won't regret this."

The wry expression on Theresa's face betrayed how she pretty much already regretted the arrangement, but she didn't say anything.

"Call the IT department," Simon instructed Mary, who seemed to be watching the interaction with frank curiosity rather than pitching in to help. Maybe someone needed to explain the teamwork concept to her. "Tell them to replace this unit and send the invoice to me through the medical staff office."

"Simon, that's really not necessary," Theresa interjected. "The ED budget can handle the replacement of a keyboard and monitor. Hopefully the hard drive is still intact."

"Let me know if it isn't." He turned toward Hailey. "Come on—let's get you settled in my office."

Hailey picked up the list of names, which were now barely legible as a result of being soaked with water. She wiped the list against the only dry spot on her pants leg, and then followed him back through the ED arena.

In the privacy of his office, he urged her to sit down in his chair behind the desk. "How bad is it?" he asked.

She momentarily closed her eyes. "Hurts a little," she admitted.

"I can tell that your leg hurts much more than just a little," he argued. "You stood on your injured leg, putting all your weight on it, didn't you?" When she didn't respond, he leaned forward earnestly. "You can be honest with me, Hailey. I'm on your side."

"I appreciate that, Simon. But I really am fine." She tilted her chin stubbornly and he had the wild urge to kiss her again. "Like I told Theresa, spilled water isn't the end of the world. I feel bad about the computer, though."

He could tell she was determined to downplay what had happened. He sighed and straightened. "Fine. I'll be right back with a hefty dose of ibuprofen and a dry pair of scrubs." He left before she could try to argue with him again.

As he made his way back through the ED, Bonnie came up to him, putting her hand on his arm. "I'm so sorry, Simon. I hope Hailey is all right."

For a split second the way she put her hand on his arm with such familiarity reminded him of Erica. But he quickly dismissed the unfair comparison, as he'd noticed most patient care providers had a touchy-feely approach to people. He couldn't help leaning back, as she was too close to his personal space. "She's fine, don't worry. Could have happened to anyone."

"Good. I'm so glad." Bonnie smiled and he was relieved when she dropped his arm and walked away.

He returned to his office with the promised ibuprofen, water and fresh pair of scrubs, to find Hailey already logged onto the computer, reviewing one of his patient's charts. He set the pain reliever and the water a good distance away from the keyboard. No sense in pushing their luck! She paused long enough to take the medication, reinforcing his belief that she hurt worse than she was letting on.

"Do you need anything else?" he asked.

"No, thanks." She flashed another strained smile, but then immediately turned her attention back to the chart. "I'll have these chart reviews finished as soon as possible."

"Hailey, take your time. There's no rush." He stood there for a moment, but as he couldn't come up with any other reason to hang around, he turned to leave.

"Simon?"

The way Hailey said his name caused an immediate physical response. One he really needed to get control over, and quickly. He paused at the doorway, and then turned to glance at her over his shoulder. "Yes?"

"Thanks for supporting me with Theresa," she said slowly. "If you hadn't, I don't think she would have let me stay on. I owe you one, Simon, big time."

You owe me, Simon. Don't leave like this. You owe me!

He blanched, echoes of his disastrous relationship with Erica reverberating through his mind. "No! You don't owe me anything," His tone came across more harshly than he'd intended. "Nothing! Understand?"

She stared at him in shock. "No, Simon. I don't understand. If you don't want my gratitude, why did you bother sticking up for me in the first place? Out of guilt? I already told you the accident wasn't your fault. I don't need your pity. I can handle things just fine on my own."

"I'm not helping you out of guilt," he protested, even though he suspected that it was, in fact, part of the reason. He struggled to get a grip. His issues with Erica and his mistakes of the past had nothing to do with

Hailey, none of this was her fault. He tried to soften his tone. "I shouldn't have snapped at you. Chalk it up to lack of sleep."

She arched a brow at him, as if she didn't believe a word he was saying.

He tried to smile but his face felt frozen. "I'll come back to check on you later, all right?"

"Don't bother," she muttered.

He opened his mouth to argue again, and then realized he should quit before he only made matters worse. "I'll see you later," he said. He left, closing the office door behind him with a sense of relief.

When he walked back into the arena, he became keenly aware of several curious pairs of eyes focused on him. He stifled the urge to shout at them to mind their own business. But he knew, better than most, how working in the emergency department was equivalent to living in a fishbowl.

That was exactly why he needed to stay away from Hailey.

No matter how desperately he wanted to see her again.

Hailey managed to get some work done, although it wasn't easy. Simon's scent permeated the office and while she was undeniably annoyed with him, she couldn't seem to prise him out of her mind.

Thanks to the ibuprofen he'd brought for her, the sharp pain in her leg had receded to a dull ache. After he'd finally left her alone, she'd gratefully changed into dry scrubs, wincing with the effort. Stupid of her to forget about her broken leg when she'd jumped up from her seat like that. Maybe she was cursed. It certainly seemed as if she was experiencing an unusual run of bad luck.

Once she was dry and feeling a little better, she went back to work, completing several of the chart reviews. One in particular bothered her. It seemed as if one of the physicians had totally missed several key symptoms on a patient, who had returned to the emergency department a couple of days later, only to end up emergently intubated and in the ICU. She placed her notes for that chart review on top, so Simon would see them right away.

When her four hours were up—Theresa had made it clear she could only work four hours a day and not a minute more—she logged off Simon's computer, feeling at least somewhat of a sense of accomplishment. Certainly completing chart reviews was better than sitting around at home all day, doing nothing.

It wasn't until she picked up her purse that she remembered Simon had given her a ride to the hospital. And she needed a way to get back home.

After the odd reaction he'd had when she'd tried to thank him earlier, she was loath to seek him out now.

He was obviously afraid she expected something from him. After that kiss down by the lakefront her attempt to thank him for his efforts had freaked him out.

She might be having a run of bad luck, but she wasn't pathetic enough to think that one kiss between two adults carried any sort of importance.

No, there was no way in the world she was going to wait around for Simon. And because Rachel was working too, her friend wasn't able to drive her home either.

Mentally she debated her options. Crutch-walking three miles to her apartment was not a smart choice. She'd thought she was in relatively good shape but soon discovered going long distances on crutches made her upper arms ache. She could call a taxi, but taking taxis to and from work each day would defeat the purpose of saving up money in order to pay her rent and the rest of her bills.

Before she'd bought her bike, she'd mapped out the bus routes to and from the hospital. The biggest problem with the bus routes in Cedar Bluff was that they weren't at the most convenient locations. At least, not for her. The closest bus stop to her apartment was a good four blocks away. And the bus stop here at the hospital was also several blocks down the road. At the time, riding her bike had been the best answer all around.

However, the bus was probably her only viable option now that she couldn't ride her bike. Surely the more she used the crutches, the more strength she'd gain in her arms?

For a moment she considered going to find Simon to let him know her plans, but she instantly dismissed the idea. He'd said he'd come back to check on things, but he hadn't.

No doubt, he was looking for ways to avoid being alone with her. She understood he didn't want her to get the wrong idea about their...*friendship*.

She was a capable adult, one who could certainly find her own way home.

The bus stop was located at the farthest corner of

the road that came right up to the main lobby, so she left the emergency department through the back way, taking the long, winding corridor down to the main lobby. From there, she slowly made her way down the street to the bus stop. Thankfully it was nice outside, if a little breezy, and not raining.

Impossible to carry an umbrella and use crutches at the same time.

After glancing at her watch, she realized she had no idea when the bus was due to arrive. With a sigh she lowered herself down onto the bus stop bench, grateful to take the pressure off her arms even for a short while.

She had no idea how much of a time lag there was between buses. Thirty minutes? Forty? Surely not more than an hour?

She should have brought something to read. Sitting around doing nothing was going to drive her crazy. An hour would feel like an eternity.

Ten minutes into her wait, a familiar low-slung black car pulled up in the bus lane. The passenger window was lowered, revealing Simon's dark scowl as he leaned over the passenger seat from the driver's side to talk to her. "What in the world are you doing out here?"

"Isn't it obvious?" she asked mildly. "Can't you see this is a bus stop? If you're looking for the quality review report, I left it on top of your desk."

If anything, his scowl deepened. "Hailey, don't be ridiculous. I'm not here for the stupid report. Get in the car. I'll drive you home."

"No, thanks."

The way Simon scrubbed his hands over his face would have been comical if she weren't so annoyed with him.

"Hailey, please. I'm going right past your house on my way home. Let me give you a lift."

She knew she should simply ignore him, but there were already a couple of cars coming up behind Simon, waiting impatiently. Simon completely ignored them, as if he couldn't care less how he was blocking the lane. One of them leaned on their horn.

Simon didn't even glance behind him, but waited patiently, looking at her expectantly. When the driver hit the horn the second time, she caved in. "Fine." She stood up, grabbed her crutches and crossed over the sidewalk to yank open the passenger door. Simon took the crutches from her and tucked them into the backseat as she slid in beside him.

Neither one of them spoke, not a single word, as he drove the few miles to her apartment building. Hailey had to admit that somehow riding in a car with Simon wasn't bad at all.

Maybe she was slowly getting over her stupid fears.

Even once they'd arrived, Simon simply hauled the crutches out of the backseat, before coming around to help her out of the car.

"You know I would have been fine on the bus," she said, when Simon followed her up to the front door of the apartment building. "But thanks for the ride."

She was surprised when he followed her inside and up the elevator to the second floor. When they reached her apartment, he waited patiently as she dug out her keys and then held the door open for her.

She blocked the doorway. "Thanks, Simon, but I'll be fine from here."

"I'd like to stay, just for a few minutes, if you'd give me a chance to explain," he said, finally breaking his prolonged silence.

Exhausted mentally and physically, she was half-tempted to tell him to take a hike. But obviously something was bothering him. She knew, both from personal experience and from Rachel, that Simon was the most even-tempered of the emergency physicians on staff at Cedar Bluff.

Reluctantly, she made her way over to the sofa, sinking gratefully onto the soft cushions. She lightly massaged her upper arms. Simon closed the door behind him, and then took a seat on the opposite end of the sofa, as far from her as possible.

"I'm sorry that I've been a jerk," he said, staring down at his feet. "You already know how I was in a relationship that ended badly."

"Yes." Hadn't they already covered this issue? She wasn't in the mood to regurgitate the past yet again. "And I already explained that I don't expect anything from you, Simon."

"I knew you didn't wait for me because you were mad. And I can't blame you."

She held up a hand to stop him. "I'm not mad. And there was no need for you to come and pick me up from the bus stop. I'm perfectly capable of taking the bus to and from work every day."

"Hailey, give me a moment to explain, would you?" He sounded exasperated.

She rolled her eyes and waved a hand, indicating he should continue.

His resigned gaze met hers. "The relationship I was in before, the one that didn't end well, involved a nurse. A nurse I worked with closely in the emergency department at Chicago's Children First Hospital."

She nodded in understanding. A nurse, a coworker, it explained a lot. She could see why he might be hesitant to go down that route again.

"The worst part of all was that when things ended badly between us," Simon said slowly as if the words were torn from somewhere deep in his soul, "we didn't just lose on a personal level, although that was bad enough. But, at least for me, I lost on a professional level as well. Because the horrible way things ended cost me my career."

CHAPTER TEN

THE moment the words left Simon's mouth he inwardly swore and wished he could call them back. He'd only intended to make Hailey feel better about why he'd been such a jerk. He hadn't planned on telling her all the gory details about his past relationship with Erica.

He hadn't told *anyone* the full extent of what had transpired.

"What? Your career? How?" Hailey demanded, her beautiful blue eyes snapping fire with outrage on his behalf. The way she jumped to his defense almost made him want to smile. "Just because you broke some sort of no-fraternising policy? That's ridiculous!"

He hesitated. How much should he tell her? Keeping his dark secret had been an ingrained habit for so long he wasn't even sure where to begin. Or where to stop. He couldn't tell her everything, just enough to help her to understand, to explain his behaviour.

"Not because of a policy," he finally admitted. "I was being groomed for the medical director position, a job I coveted. But one disastrous night my personal life became center stage in the middle of the ED."

"Oh, no," she whispered in horror. And she didn't

know the half of it. The personal loss was hard enough, but to have everyone else know about it was far worse.

"The scene was pretty ugly and afterwards my career suffered irreversible damage," he continued, determined to finish. "My boss pretty much came right out and told me I should look for another position at a different hospital if I wanted to move into a leadership role." Even now, that painful discussion grated on him. As much as he'd understood where his boss had been coming from, he'd found it impossible to believe his four years of hard work hadn't counted for more.

Erica had blown his dreams away in a fit of anger.

No, that wasn't fair. The entire mess had been his fault and no one else's.

Hailey's brow puckered into a frown. "I'm surprised you allowed yourself to participate in a fight with your girlfriend in the middle of the unit," she said frankly. "That's not at all your style."

Simon dropped his head and rubbed the back of his neck. He hadn't participated in the fight, other than to try to get Erica out of there when she had started screaming at him so they could talk someplace private. But that had been when she'd turned on him like a wild-cat, hitting and scratching, striking out in anger. He'd defended himself the best he could without hurting her, but in the end several nurses had been forced to step in, dragging Erica off him. Just thinking about the humiliation of that night made his gut knot painfully.

He'd handled it all wrong, he could see that so clearly now. Erica hadn't been emotionally stable, and his breaking things off had only been one issue sending her over the edge. Getting his life back on track had been hard enough, but he hadn't been given the chance to recover once Erica had resorted to other means to make him pay.

In some respects, he was still paying for his mistake.

Would he be forced to pay forever?

"Simon?" Hailey said his name, dragging his thoughts back to the present. "What happened?"

"I was caught off guard," he admitted. "I wasn't expecting her to start yelling at me in the middle of the unit, dragging our personal life into the public eye. But in the end it didn't matter who started what. I took accountability for what happened because I didn't handle things well enough with her from the very beginning."

"I see," Hailey murmured, although he could see dozens of questions reflected in her eyes that showed she really didn't.

He didn't want to go into details about Erica with Hailey. Mostly because he was too embarrassed at how far things had spiraled out of control. And the role he'd unwittingly played.

He could see now how his good intentions had only made things worse instead of better.

But the past was over and done with. He just wanted to move on. "I came to Cedar Bluff to start over. It's a great hospital and a warm, welcoming community. And for once my timing was right on target because the medical director here, George Hanover is about ready to retire and I've made it clear I'm interested in replacing him."

"I'm surprised Dr. Taylor, Dr. Reichert or Dr. Torres aren't fighting you for the spot," she pointed out, naming the other younger attending physicians on staff. Seth, Jadon and Quinn were his colleagues but he also considered them his friends. "They've been here longer than you and have more seniority."

Talking about his career was much easier than talking about his personal failures. "They have more seniority here," he agreed. "But being a medical director is more about management experience than just tenure and I have far more management experience than they do, thanks to my years at Children First in Chicago. I'm already the chairman of the ED quality review committee, which means I work closely with Theresa on cases where we could have done better either from a medical or nursing perspective."

Hailey smiled warmly. "It's no wonder you're such a great doctor. I can tell you really care about your work, Simon."

He shrugged, pleased with the compliment. Because she was right. His patients were important to him. Although somewhere along the line, his personal life had become important too.

"I do. Very much." Which was why he was trying so hard to keep his distance from Hailey. To ignore his unwavering physical attraction to her. His expression turned serious. "I'm sorry Hailey, but I hope you can see where I'm coming from. I can't afford to screw up this opportunity."

Her smile faded and she dropped her gaze. "I understand, Simon. Although, I've already tried to explain that I'm not interested in having a romantic relationship with you."

Her blunt statement stabbed deep. He ignored the

pain, telling himself this was exactly what he wanted. So the kiss they'd shared didn't mean as much to her as it had to him. Fine. Better for both of them. "Good. Then we're in agreement. I hope we can remain friends."

The expression in her gaze was difficult to read but she readily agreed. "Of course. Friends."

There was a long, awkward silence. Time to change the subject to something neutral. He glanced around. "Ah, what time do you work tomorrow?" he asked.

She lifted a shoulder. "I can go in anytime, as long as I get the work done. Theresa made it clear I could only work four hours a day, regardless. Apparently they don't want me to overdo things."

"Sounds reasonable to me."

She grimaced. "I'd rather work full-time, but after that mess today, I'm just grateful Theresa is willing to keep me on at all."

He could relate. "I work day shift tomorrow, but I could come over right after work to pick you up," he offered.

But she was already shaking her head. "No, thanks, I would rather take the bus in."

He didn't understand the flare of panic. Was this it then? Was she going to stop seeing him completely? He'd been banking on the fact that they'd continue to spend time together at least as friends.

Quickly, he considered his options. "Actually, that would work out great, Hailey. Why don't you come in around eleven? You can use my office since I'll be staffing in the department, caring for patients, and then I can drive you home after my shift is over."

For a moment she looked like she might argue, but

then she slowly nodded. "Sure, that might work. I'll see how I feel in the morning."

For a moment he wondered if she was just stringing him along, but then he pushed the idea aside. Surely Hailey wasn't looking forward to riding the bus. While she was on crutches he wanted to help in any way possible.

His stomach rumbled and he realized they'd missed lunch. "Are you hungry? There's a Chinese place nearby that delivers."

She looked taken aback by his suggestion. "I was planning to relax and watch a movie tonight. Really, Simon, you don't have to stick around to entertain me. I'll be fine."

"I need to eat too and I don't have any plans for the evening," he assured her, getting up from the sofa and pulling out his cell phone. "And luckily I have Chang Lee's number in my cell phone directory. Chang Lee's has the best Chinese food in town. Anything in particular you want to eat or should I get a variety?"

There was a pause and he waited, hoping she wouldn't tell him to get lost. "A variety."

He couldn't help but grin. It was nice to have a woman who shared his taste in food. Erica had been the queen of eating salads. Except she hadn't eaten them, she'd picked at them. Had driven him nuts. "Perfect."

He gave their order to Mrs. Chang Lee herself, and then picked up the movies she had sitting on top of the DVD player. They were both romantic comedies, but as he'd invited himself over, he wasn't about to complain. "Which one did you plan on watching?" he asked.

"*The Princess Bride*," she said instantly. "It's my favorite."

He'd never watched it, but tried not to grimace at her selection. He was sure he wouldn't like the chick flick, but staying there with Hailey for a few hours watching something he didn't like was better than going home to sit in his empty house all alone.

His cell phone rang, and he glanced at the screen, wondering who was calling. He frowned when he saw *Unidentified number* on the display.

Every day for the past week he'd had hang-up messages on his answering-machine at home. Up to five a day. He figured the telemarketers would give up sooner or later.

But would telemarketers call on his cell phone? He pushed the button to send the caller to voice mail. The caller with the unidentified number could just leave a message.

A few minutes later his phone chirped again, announcing he had a voice mail message. Planning to listen to it later, he tucked his phone away.

He loaded the movie into the DVD player. Ten minutes into the movie, their food arrived. They ate while they watched, and he hated to admit that the movie wasn't nearly as bad as he'd anticipated.

Sappy, sure. But enough action to make up for it.

There was only about six inches of space between them on the sofa as Hailey had stretched out in her search for comfort, her broken leg propped up on several pillows. Her eyelids drooped, as if she was exhausted.

He seriously considered pulling her into his arms,

knowing she'd be far more comfortable, but instantly rejected the idea. He was the one who'd set the boundary of friendship. So he kept his gaze on the movie, subtly watching her out of the corner of his eye.

Very soon her head dipped down to the right, her chin practically resting on her chest.

Her breathing evened out and he realized with an amused grin that she'd fallen asleep. When she slid further toward him, he debated only a moment before drawing her close, so she could rest without suffering a crick in her neck.

She turned her face into the hollow of his shoulder. He held his breath, waiting. Was she awake? When she didn't move for several long moments, he bent to lightly rest his cheek on the top of her head. Her scent filled his senses and he nearly groaned when his body tightened with need.

He ignored the urge to kiss her awake. Maybe, if the stars were aligned in his favor, she'd stay close to him like this for a while.

Pathetic, sure, but he was willing to take what little bit he could get.

When the movie was over, he didn't want to disturb her so he used the remote to change the channel to a ball game. Luckily, there was a double header playing. He put the sound on mute and watched the action silently.

But he couldn't have told anyone who won the game. Soon he closed his eyes, and held Hailey in his arms as she slept, secretly wishing things could be different.

Wishing he deserved a personal relationship—a future with someone like Hailey.

* * *

Hailey gradually became aware of her surroundings, realizing very quickly from the deep rumble beneath her ear that she was not alone.

Sucking in a quick breath, she froze and became instantly wide awake, blinking in the dimness of the room.

Simon was holding her in his arms. A soft snoring sound filled the air, confirming he'd fallen asleep. There was some old black and white sitcom flickering across the television screen and from what she could see out of her living-room window the night was pitch black.

She guessed the time to be well after midnight.

How on earth had this happened? The last thing she remembered was watching *The Princess Bride*. But not the end, she realized with a frown. Darn it, she'd missed her favorite part.

Holding herself still, she breathed in Simon's musky scent, enjoying the feeling of being pressed up against him a little too much.

She should wake him up and send him on his way. Sleeping in Simon's arms was not in keeping with their deal.

Friendship. All he wanted from her was friendship.

After hearing about what had happened in his previous relationship, and how his personal life had ruined his career, she really couldn't blame him for not wanting to get personally involved.

There had been a tiny part of her that had wanted to protest, telling him she was not like his ex-girlfriend. She'd never start a fight with him in the middle of the emergency department.

After all, she worked there, too.

Since the flashbacks after her bike accident hadn't

returned, she'd hoped that she'd successfully put the past to rest. Although, if she was honest, she'd admit the familiar cloak of guilt remained.

She wasn't the right woman for Simon. He could do far better. She knew he could easily find someone else. Someone worthy of his love. Possibly someone who didn't work with him in the emergency department.

But maybe, just for a brief time, enjoying what they had would be heavenly. Because being with Simon like this, in his arms, however accidentally, made her feel alive.

Steeling her resolve to get up, putting an end to the ridiculous fantasies, she placed her hand on his chest and gently pushed herself upward.

Simon's arm tightened around her, holding her in place. "Hailey," he murmured.

Her breath lodged in her throat. Was he dreaming about her? The way she'd dreamed about him?

No, maybe he was awake. "Simon," she whispered. "We have to get up. We fell asleep."

In the dim light of the TV she saw his eyes were open and he was staring at her intently. He shifted and suddenly she was lying more fully against him.

She sucked in another breath, acutely aware of the rigid hardness of his groin pressing against her.

"Hailey," he said again, his tone husky and pleading at the same time. Before she could respond, he lowered his head and kissed her.

She fisted her hand in his shirt to push him away, but when he angled his head to deepen the kiss she lost the battle with her common sense. With a groan she returned his kiss, eagerly pressing against him, desperate for more.

She didn't want to be Simon's friend.

She wanted him like this. Holding her and kissing her like he'd never let go.

The heat of his hand scorched the bare skin of her back when he slid it beneath the thin fabric of her loose top. She nearly wept with intense pleasure.

Too long. Fourteen long months since she'd been held like this. Kissed like this.

Made love to like this.

She shifted to the side, giving him better access to her breasts. Her hand lowered and caressed the rock hardness straining against his zipper.

He groaned again, pressing deeper into her caress, but when she stroked him again more firmly he froze. She sensed he was about to pull away.

"Simon, please," she whispered, stroking him and eliciting another low groan. "Don't stop."

There was a long silence, and she hoped she'd gotten through to him, but then suddenly he pulled his hand from beneath her shirt and grasped her wrist, halting her caress. "No, Hailey. We can't do this."

For a moment she wanted to rail at him. Why was he doing this to her? First he'd said no, then he'd invited himself for dinner and then he'd fallen asleep on her sofa, holding her in his arms.

One minute he'd been kissing her and the next he was telling her they couldn't do this.

She resented feeling like a yo-yo.

With a spurt of anger she pushed away from him. She swung the leg that had the cast onto the floor and sat up, putting as much distance as possible between them. She grabbed her crutches and levered off the couch, crossing the room so she wouldn't be tempted to smack some sense into him.

"If you remember, I didn't ask you to stay, Simon," she said in a clipped tone. "You're the one who over-stayed your welcome."

He let out a heavy sigh. "I know. I'm sorry."

His apology only made her angrier. "I don't want you to be sorry, Simon! I want you to make up your mind. Are we friends? Or are we something more? Because quite frankly the signals you're sending out are so damn confusing I can't figure them out." She gripped the hand rests of her crutches tightly. "What do you want from me?"

He rose to his feet, stumbling a bit before he got his balance. "I want to be your friend, Hailey. I wish I could... But it doesn't matter. All I can offer you is friendship."

She stared at him. "I can't do this. I changed my mind," she said abruptly, swinging away and walking toward the kitchen, flipping on the light as she went. Too bad she didn't have a bottle of whiskey because right now she could use a shot. She put her crutches aside and opened the fridge, settling for a glass of orange juice instead.

"Changed your mind about what?" he asked, follow-ing more slowly. The way he limped and kept stamping his foot on the floor made her suspect his leg had fallen asleep.

Too bad. She was too upset with him to give a damn. She downed the orange juice in one gulp and then leaned against the edge of the counter, crossing her arms over her chest defensively. "I changed my mind about being your friend, Simon." Her words stopped him in mid-step. "I think it would be best for both of us if we stopped seeing each other completely."

CHAPTER ELEVEN

"No Way." Hailey was surprised at the vehemence in his tone and the stark anguish on his face. "Please don't do this. I want to help while your leg is healing. Don't throw me out of your life completely."

She stared at him. And suddenly she was tired of arguing. Obviously the only thing that was going to get through to him was the blunt truth. "I can't do this, Simon. I can't treat you like a friend when I want more from you." She took a deep breath and let it out slowly, searching for the courage to bare her soul. "I want more than friendship. I want what just happened on the sofa. And since you've made it clear you can't or won't return my feelings, it's better for me if I don't see you at all on a personal level."

For a long moment he didn't answer, myriad emotions playing across his features. But then he came closer, the rest of the way into the kitchen. She would have taken a step back, but she was already up against the kitchen counter.

"Okay," he said finally.

Okay what? He was going to leave her alone? Fine. That was exactly what she wanted. She ignored the sharp stab of disappointment, swallowed hard and tilted her chin, determined to see this through. "I'm glad you understand."

"Oh, I understand exactly where you're coming from, Hailey. Because I want you, too."

Nonplussed, she stared at him. He came closer, lightly grasping her shoulders in his hands. She opened her mouth but nothing came out.

"So you're basically telling me that it's all or nothing between us, right?" His dark eyes pierced hers. She nodded, unable to speak. His expression twisted wryly. "In that case, I choose all. Everything."

"What?" She found her voice, but it was her turn to backpedal. She'd thrown out the challenge but hadn't expected him to actually take her up on the offer. And what about his determination not to get involved with someone he worked with? She tried to gather her scattered thoughts. "But…on the sofa, you stopped…"

"I was stupid. I panicked. Give me another chance, Hailey." He nuzzled her hair, his voice low, husky. "This time I promise I won't stop."

When she pulled back to stare at him, he took her silence for acquiescence and kissed her again. Urgently. Desperately. Showing her without words how much he wanted her.

And, heaven help her, she wasn't strong enough to push him away. She slipped her arms around his neck, drawing him closer. The endless kiss was only broken by the all-too-human need to breathe.

"I can't let you go after all, Hailey," he murmured. "Don't ask me to."

His confession made her heart swell with hope. When he swung her into his arms she gasped, realizing his intent. "Simon, are you sure about this? I won't—I won't quit my job for you."

"We'll need to be discreet," he said, planting a kiss on her temple as he strode confidently down the hall to her bedroom. "And careful. Neither one of us is going to quit our jobs, but we need to keep our personal feelings out of the workplace. But no matter what, I can't walk away, Hailey. I can't imagine leaving you."

"But—" she tried again.

"Don't. Let's just take this one step at a time, hmm?"

Making love seemed like a giant leap rather than a single step, but when he gently set her on the bed and began to strip off his clothes, she couldn't find the strength to protest.

Naked, he was simply amazing, all hard sculpted muscles and lean hips. When he reached for the hem of her scrub top, drawing it slowly up and over her head, she quelled a spurt of panic. She hadn't been with a man in years, not since Andrew.

"God, Hailey, you're so beautiful," he whispered huskily nuzzling the valley between her breasts after he tossed her bra aside. "I don't deserve you."

That made her laugh. If only he knew. "Oh, Simon. I don't deserve you, either."

His eyes glittered in the darkness. "I guess that means we're perfect for each other."

She wasn't so sure that was true, but when he kissed her again, following her down onto the mattress, their naked limbs entwined, she gave herself up to the wonderful sensations. When he kissed his way down her body, exploring every inch, she stopped thinking at all.

No matter what happened between them, she wouldn't regret one moment of being with him like this.

Simon prised his eyes open, instinctively knowing it was time for him to get up. His internal alarm clock never failed him and when he blinked the sleep from his eyes, glancing at Hailey's clock on her dresser, he saw it was five in the morning. Just enough time to get home, shower, change and then get to work.

Hailey murmured in protest when he untangled himself from the bed. "Shh," he murmured. "Go back to sleep." He soothed her with a gentle kiss.

She nodded, obviously half-asleep as she snuggled deeper beneath the covers, and he had to fight the urge to join her. He stood staring at her for a long time, knowing he was crazy to have stayed to make love to her but unable to deny a surge of satisfaction.

No matter what, he couldn't regret making love to Hailey. She'd been so good for him. No, actually, they'd been good for each other. For the first time in what seemed like for ever, the future didn't seem quite so bleak. Or lonely.

Only the knowledge that he'd see her in a few hours made it possible for him to turn away and pull on his wrinkled clothes, moving quietly as he let himself out of her apartment.

He made it to work early, heading to his office so he could review the quality report Hailey had left for him. When he used the key in the lock, though, his door opened easily.

With a frown, he realized Hailey couldn't have locked

it behind her. Probably because he'd promised to return to check on things.

When he flipped on the light, his desk was neat and tidy. But there was no report. Hadn't Hailey told him she'd leave it on top of his desk?

He opened the top drawer and the side drawers, wondering if she'd meant to leave it out but had, in fact, tucked it away instead. But he didn't find anything.

Not even in the garbage.

Perplexed, he sat at his desk, staring at the computer screen. He didn't know what had happened to the report, but all he could do was to wait for Hailey to come in. No doubt she'd know where to find it.

He quickly reviewed his email, responding to the various issues before heading back into the trauma bay for the start of his shift.

"Hey, Simon. How are you?" Quinn Torres greeted him when he walked in.

"I'm good, thanks. How was your night?"

Quinn shrugged. "Not bad. Leila and I didn't have too many trauma admissions."

Simon had been a bit surprised to discover that Quinn often matched up his shifts in the ED with the nights his wife, Leila, who was one of the trauma surgeons, happened to be on call. Apparently they weren't worried about working together. In fact, they seemed to enjoy it.

A kernel of doubt gnawed at him, but he shoved it aside. Hailey was the complete opposite of Erica. She was fiercely independent and adorably stubborn. They'd both been on the exact same page last night. He flat out refused to regret taking their relationship to the next level. "How's Danny?" he asked, focusing on Quinn.

"He's good," Quinn responded with a broad grin. Once his son Danny had had emotional issues that had prevented him from talking, but not any more. "He's thrilled because we let him spend the night with Ben Taylor."

The two boys had been inseparable, even in those early days when Danny hadn't been talking. He remembered how Hailey had suspected Seth of hurting Ben. If only she knew how much they were all like one big family.

One in which he'd often played the outsider, looking in.

"I bet they had a blast," Simon agreed. He glanced up at the census board and the dozen or so names that were still listed there. "Give me the rundown on the patients so you can get out of here."

When Quinn had finished going through the patients that were still in the ED, Leila arrived, walking toward them and wrapping her arms around her husband's waist in a tight hug. "Ready, darling?" she asked.

"Absolutely," he responded huskily, and the way the two gazed into each other's eyes made it clear they were heading home to bed but not to sleep.

Simon flashed a wry grin, for once not experiencing the pang of envy he usually felt when watching the married couples around him. Maybe because he'd spent a rather satisfying night with Hailey?

And he hoped they'd have many more. The mere thought made him grin.

"Get out of here," Simon said, shooing them away. "I have work to do."

The four hours dragged by with excruciating slowness as he examined and treated patients. He was standing in the arena when Hailey walked in.

"Good morning," she greeted him in a reserved tone, abiding by her promise to keep things professional while they were at work. "Do you have a list of patients you need reviewed today?"

"Actually, I need the reviews you did yesterday," he told her.

Her eyes widened in surprise. "What are you talking about?" she demanded with a frown. "I left the details of my review right on top of your desk."

Several employees, two nurses and the unit clerk were watching their interaction with open curiosity. His face tightened and he gave a jerky nod toward his office. "Let's discuss this in private," he said in a clipped tone.

She followed him into the office, and then stopped abruptly when she saw the empty desktop. "I don't understand. I swear, Simon, I left the report right there on the top of your desk."

He let out a sigh. "Well it's obviously not here, Hailey. Go and check your locker. Maybe you intended to leave it here but took it with you by mistake."

"I didn't take it with me." Her blue eyes flashed fire and he couldn't help thinking about how beautiful she looked, even when she was angry. "Carrying things with my crutches isn't exactly easy. I didn't take the report out of the office. I know I left it here, Simon. Someone must have taken it. I left your door open because I wasn't sure whether you had your keys and I didn't want to lock you out."

He remembered how his office door hadn't been locked. In his haste to find Hailey last night, he'd simply closed the door behind him without checking. "You're right, my door wasn't locked. But I've searched everywhere, in the desk drawers, even in the garbage, and it's not here."

"Someone must have taken it."

He snorted. "Oh, sure, that makes sense. Why on earth would someone take it, Hailey? What's the point? The report isn't irreplaceable. You can re-create it easily enough."

She slowly shook her head. "I don't know, Simon. But I still think it's odd. I can't help but wonder if someone took it to make me look incompetent."

Hailey stewed over the missing report long after she'd re-created it and moved on to the next few cases.

She wasn't losing her mind. She'd left the report in plain view. Someone had to have taken it on purpose. To make her look bad?

She couldn't help remembering the way the ED tech, Bonnie, had tripped and spilled water all over her the day before. Had that been on purpose too? But if so, why? Bonnie was relatively new to Cedar Bluff, just like she was. Why would the tech dislike her so much? She couldn't remember having had any sort of run-in with the woman.

Hailey hadn't been in Cedar Bluff long enough to make enemies. She'd barely had time to make friends in the two months since she'd started.

She pushed the paranoid thoughts aside. Maybe the answer was something simple. Like the papers had fallen on the floor and the cleaning staff had tossed them out because they'd thought they were garbage.

That must be it. There wasn't some sort of conspiracy against her.

She focused her attention on completing the list Simon had given her. Even when her four hours were up, she kept working. At a quarter to four Simon opened the office door. "Hailey? Are you ready to go?"

"No. I need to finish this report first."

He leaned against the doorjamb, frowning at her. "I thought Theresa didn't want you to work more than four hours?"

"I'm not counting the first thirty minutes it took me to re-create the missing review. As far as I'm concerned, the clock started at noon." She barely glanced at him, intent on getting the last chart finished. "Go ahead and leave if you want. I'll take the bus home."

She heard him sigh. "Finish your report, then. I'll give you fifteen minutes." Her shoulders dropped in relief when he stepped back and closed the door.

For a moment she allowed herself the luxury of dropping her head into her hands and massaging her temples. Treating Simon like a stranger at work was more difficult than she'd imagined.

Last night, making love with Simon had been incredible. Better than anything she could possibly dream up. But now, in the cold light of day, nagging doubts threatened to choke her.

Maybe they were moving too fast. Maybe they needed

to take a step back and really think about what they were doing.

Already, it seemed as if keeping their personal lives separate from their professional lives would be next to impossible. From the moment she'd come into the unit, she'd been able to feel Simon's terseness as he'd asked about the report. She'd been taken completely off guard at his annoyance after the wonderful night they'd shared.

With a deep, cleansing breath, she lifted her head and went back to reading the electronic chart. She made several notations and then sat back, rubbing the back of her neck.

She was finished, with five minutes to spare.

It was tempting to leave now, before Simon returned. But when she glanced down at the stack of papers containing all her notes, she scowled.

No way. This time she wasn't leaving until Simon had the reviews safely in his hands.

While she waited she gazed curiously around his office. He had his medical school diploma and his undergraduate diploma mounted proudly on the wall. But other than those two items, there was nothing personal that she could see.

Not even one photo of his family.

She frowned. Did Simon have family? Surely he had parents somewhere. But the question bothered her. She'd slept with the man but she didn't really know much about him.

Other than the fact that he had a former girlfriend who'd started a huge fight in the emergency department, which had cost him his job.

Why was the lack of knowledge about Simon's family bothering her now? She'd thought she'd known Andrew very well, had met his family numerous times, but in the end the way he'd started to drink heavily had been a surprise.

The office door opened, startling her. "All finished?" Simon asked.

"Yes." She leaned on the desk to stand, balancing her weight on her good leg. She held out the stack of paperwork she'd compiled. "You might want to put this someplace safe."

He came into the room, taking the paperwork from her and leafing through it quickly. "Very comprehensive, Hailey," he commented. "Thanks."

"You're welcome." She reached for her crutches.

Simon edged behind her—the office really wasn't very big—and opened his desk drawer, putting the paperwork she'd handed him into one of his files.

"Aren't you going to lock it?" she asked, when he slammed the drawer shut.

"No. I'll make sure the office door is locked."

Hailey frowned. "Humor me. Lock the desk, too. The cleaning people have a key to your office, right?"

"Yeah, probably."

"If the cleaning staff has a set of keys, then pretty much anyone could get one if they really wanted to. Maybe someone on staff doesn't like the idea of me reviewing the care of our patients. Maybe they're afraid we might find something they'd missed."

He paused, but then slowly nodded. "I'd thought of that possibility too," he admitted. "Okay, I'll lock the desk."

She stood by the doorway as he searched for and found the keys to the desk. Once he'd locked everything up, he put the key on his keyring.

Awkwardly, she leaned on one crutch to open the door. Simon came up behind her, and placed his hand in the small of her back. "I'll get it," he said, his voice close to her ear.

His touch, even as light as it was, sent fissures of awareness tingling down her spine.

She blushed, wondering if he had any idea what he was doing to her. "Simon, maybe you should wait here and let me go first, so it doesn't look so obviously like we're leaving together."

"Don't be ridiculous," Simon responded, but he dropped his hand from her back as he opened the door wider. "Everyone knows I hit you on your bike. It's no secret that I feel responsible. Giving you a ride home isn't a big deal."

She swallowed her argument, her expression annoyed as she swung out of the office on her crutches. Why the man was so stubborn was beyond her.

Maybe it was just her imagination, but it seemed like everyone in the arena stopped what they were doing and blatantly stared at her as she came out of Simon's office and walked across the unit.

This was exactly what she'd been afraid of. She imagined the rumors about Simon and herself were flying fast and furious.

"Hailey, watch out!"

Too late. She belatedly realized water was on the floor when the crutch in her right hand slid out from beneath her.

CHAPTER TWELVE

SIMON leaped forward as Hailey leaned heavily on one crutch, precariously teetering as she struggled to keep her balance.

The crutch clattered to the floor.

"I've got you," he said, catching her and hauling her close in time to prevent her from falling.

"Thanks," she murmured, her voice muffled by his shirt.

For a moment he almost forgot they were standing in the middle of the arena, so overcome was he by the urge to kiss her. But he managed to loosen his grip and take a safe step backward. "Okay now?"

"Of course." Hailey pointedly averted her gaze as she stood leaning on one crutch. Simon bent down to pick up the other one, which had crashed to the floor. She took it wordlessly.

"Call Housekeeping and get someone over here to mop up the spill," Simon directed the unit clerk, the one with the weird green eyes. "And throw me a towel, please."

"I already called them," Mary assured him, her expression one of concern. He grabbed the towel from Bonnie and placed it over the spill.

"Good thing you're so quick," Bonnie said, "otherwise poor Hailey might have fallen and hurt herself even worse."

"Yeah." He carefully stepped around the wet spot on the floor, wondering why it seemed Hailey was suddenly so accident prone. Especially when the accidents were not the result of anything she'd done.

If you didn't count riding her bike in a thunderstorm.

Simon hurried after Hailey as she'd continued crossing the arena, heading for the hallway leading to the staff locker rooms. He caught up with her right before she disappeared inside. "Hailey? Are you all right?"

"I'm fine." Her low voice was difficult to read. "I'll meet you outside in the parking lot in a few minutes."

He stepped back, frowning as she disappeared into the woman's locker room. Had she hurt herself but was afraid to say anything? He was tempted to follow her inside, but forced himself to head out to his car.

True to her word, Hailey came out less than five minutes later. She had her purse slung over her shoulder, and this time she put her crutches in the back herself, before sliding into the passenger seat.

He didn't immediately drive away. "Are you sure you're all right?" he asked. "Did you wrench your arm or your shoulder?"

"No, luckily my arm strength has improved over the past week." Hailey relaxed against the seat with a sigh. "But I swear I'm cursed."

"I doubt you're cursed, Hailey," he muttered. "But it does seem as if you've had a run of bad luck. I'm glad you didn't hurt yourself."

"Me, too. Where are we going?" she asked, when he turned left instead of right toward her apartment.

"I thought maybe we'd go out for dinner," he said, keeping his tone casual with an effort. He felt guilty for not taking her out on a proper date before spending the night in her apartment. He glanced over at her, trying to gauge her reaction. "Is that all right with you?"

"Ah, sure." Hailey flashed him a tentative smile. "Dinner sounds good."

He relaxed a bit. At least she hadn't told him to take a hike. "There's a nice restaurant, Stephen's, that over-looks the harbor."

"Would you mind if we took a walk first?" Hailey asked, when he pulled into the parking lot of Stephen's. "I really need to stretch my muscles. I'm not used to sitting so much. I miss my bike," she said in a forlorn tone.

He almost laughed, but then realized she was serious. "So you really enjoy riding your bike everywhere?" he asked curiously. He couldn't imagine functioning without a car.

"Yeah, I do." Hailey turned onto the sidewalk that ran along the lakeshore. "I don't particularly like exercising in general, especially running, but biking helps to keep me in shape."

He thought of the bike he'd purchased last summer. He'd only ridden it once, and that had been for a charity ride that a group of the ED doctors had participated in. His butt had hurt for almost a week after a measly twenty-five-mile ride. "I have a bike," he told her. "Maybe once you're off your crutches we can ride together."

She threw him a surprised glance and nodded. "Sure."

The wind kicked up, bringing a cool breeze off the lake. When Hailey shivered, he suggested they turn around and head inside.

Since they were still rather early, they had their choice of seating. Simon asked for a table overlooking the harbor.

"It's so beautiful," Hailey murmured, staring through the window at the purple and pink sky. He took the crutches from her, propping them against the wall, and then held the chair for her. "Thanks."

"Would you like something to drink?" Simon asked, opening the menu to review the appetizers.

"Just water for me," Hailey said as she read through the menu.

"Not a glass of wine? Or a cocktail?" he asked. Didn't she realize he was trying to make up for his lapse of not asking her out sooner? "I'm driving," he teased.

She frowned and shook her head. "Actually, Simon, I don't drink. At all. And if you don't mind, I'd rather you didn't drink tonight either as you are driving."

Surprised, he stared at her. Was she joking? Surely one drink couldn't hurt either of them. But then he understood. "Because of the accident?"

She stared at her menu for so long he thought she wasn't going to answer him. Finally she dragged her gaze up to his. "Yes. Andrew had had several martinis that night and I could tell he wasn't in any condition to drive, so I told him I would. Unfortunately, he didn't think he was impaired and kept insisting he wanted to drive. We argued, not just in the parking lot but even after he finally gave me the keys and we started driving home." There was a brief pause. "I couldn't let it go."

She looked so stricken his heart went out to her. "And then what happened?"

Her voice had dropped down so low he was forced to lean forward to hear her. "On the way home, a truck came out of nowhere. I was so busy arguing with Andrew I didn't see the truck until it was too late. He ran a red light, striking the passenger side of our car."

She looked as if she was about to burst into tears. "It's okay, Hailey," he said, reaching across the table to take her hand. He wished they were at home so he could hold her in his arms. "I'm here for you."

"I don't think you understand. Andrew died because of me." Hailey raised her anguished gaze up to his. "Don't you see? If I hadn't argued with him, if I hadn't made such a big deal out of it, he'd be alive right now."

"No, you don't know that," he argued, tightening his grip on her hand when she tried to pull away. "Hailey, listen to me. So you argued. So what? The guy ran a red light! How is that in any way your fault?"

"I didn't see him. I wasn't paying close enough attention to my surroundings," she said.

"And you think if Andrew had been driving, the outcome would have been any better? That's crazy. For sure he wouldn't have been able to pay close attention to his surroundings, not after all those drinks. No, I think if Andrew had been driving, both of you would have probably died."

She was quiet for a long moment. "I've replayed those seconds before the crash over and over in my head. I just can't help thinking I should have seen that red truck sooner."

"And if you had?" he pressed. "Was there really a way to avoid the guy running a red light? Seriously, Hailey, where could you have gone? You had the right of way, didn't you?"

She shrugged helplessly.

He couldn't stand to see her hurting like this. Why had he brought up the painful past? But then a horrible thought occurred to him. "You did have the right of way, correct? I mean, you didn't get a ticket or anything, did you?" he asked cautiously.

"No." Hailey let out a deep heavy sigh. "He got the ticket, not me. But just a few weeks later I heard about another woman who was having an argument in the car and caused a serious accident. She got cited for reckless homicide. Ever since then I've wondered if I got off too easy."

Hailey couldn't believe she'd told Simon her deepest secret, but now that it was out in the open, she couldn't deny feeling relieved.

"Trust me, Hailey, a guy running a red light trumps an argument in the car every time." Simon stroked his thumb over the back of her hand, the caress sending tingles of awareness up her arm. "I heard about that case where the woman was cited for reckless homicide for not paying attention to the road because it made national news, but that was a completely different situation. Don't you see? It wasn't your inattentiveness that caused the accident, the way it did with that woman. The guy who ran the red light broke the law and caused the accident."

She licked her suddenly dry lips. What he was saying did make sense. But she'd lived with the guilt for so long she was afraid to believe. "I wish I could believe that for sure, Simon. Every time I think of that night, I think of how I might have punched the gas pedal, shooting forward enough to avoid the crash if I hadn't been so busy arguing with Andrew about his drinking."

"Don't torture yourself like this," he pleaded. "I'm sorry you had to go through that but you can't feel guilty for the rest of your life. I've felt guilty over things I've done in the past, too, but sometimes I think bad things happen for a reason. Because they teach us a lesson. Or because they somehow make us stronger."

He wasn't telling her anything she hadn't already told herself. Because there were times that she wondered how Andrew would have turned out if he had survived. Would he have continued to drink? Become an alcoholic? Or would he have turned his life around? Could she have helped him?

It was the not knowing that hurt the worst.

But one thing she did know for sure. In her heart, she knew that she and Andrew hadn't been destined to stay together.

"I guess you're right," she agreed slowly. For the first time she considered how the accident might have made her stronger. For one thing, she'd learned how to overcome adversity in a big way.

Was it possible Simon was right? That things happened for a reason?

It occurred to her suddenly that if she hadn't been

riding her bike in the thunderstorm because of her fear of driving, she and Simon might not be sitting across from each other right now.

Fate? Maybe.

The waiter interrupted them, asking if they'd decided on what they wanted to order. She was very glad when Simon turned down the happy-hour cocktail two-for-one specials to order the tomato and mozzarella appetizer instead. He also told the waiter to keep their water glasses full.

"Thank you, Simon," she said, after the waiter left.

"For what?" he asked, reaching for her hand again.

"Not drinking," she clarified. "I know I'm probably overreacting, but after everything that happened with Andrew, I can't help how I feel."

"Hailey, you are far more important to me than a measly drink," he said in a low, husky tone. "Of course I'm going to honor your wishes. Why wouldn't I?"

She had to blink to keep sudden tears from welling up in her eyes. She remembered, with sudden clarity, how she'd pleaded with Andrew to stop after the third martini, especially because his voice had become more boisterous and his gait unsteady, indicating he'd had enough. But he'd brushed aside her concerns as if they'd been unimportant.

She shouldn't doubt her decision not to let Andrew drive. But maybe she should have called for a taxi. Although there was no way of knowing if the taxi would have been hit by the red truck instead.

"Hailey, don't. Please." She glanced at him in surprise. And the expression in his gaze confirmed he knew exactly what was going through her mind. "Don't keep playing the what-if game. It's a game that's impossible to win."

She couldn't help but smile. "You sound like you're speaking from experience."

He nodded, his expression grimly serious. The shadows in his gaze surprised her. "I am. I've played that game too many times to count. And I lost every time."

Because of the fight with his girlfriend that had cost him his career? "Simon, you're not responsible for what's-her-name's actions. Really, what could you have done differently?"

There was a long pause. "Erica," he said finally. "Her name was Erica. And I know I'm not responsible for her actions, but I am responsible for my own."

Before she could ask him what he meant by that, the waiter brought their appetizer. From there, the conversation turned to food and the choices of possible entrées.

They each decided to try something different and to split the meals to share. Hailey was glad when Simon kept the mood of the evening light.

She couldn't remember the last time she'd had fun spending time with a man. How long since she'd been out on a date? Not since those early months with Andrew.

And she wasn't going to think of her former fiancé now.

For once she was going to be selfish and only think about herself. And Simon.

She was going to learn from her past mistakes and move forward with her life.

"Are you all finished?" he asked, when she set her fork down and pushed her plate away with a sigh.

"Yes, the food was delicious but, honestly, I can't eat another bite."

His plate was, of course, completely empty. "Neither can I. Although I can't decide which meal I liked more. Your swordfish or my veal."

She laughed. "They were both fabulous. And it looks like your mother taught you to always clean up your plate," she teased.

"She did." Simon handed over her crutches when she stood. "My parents chose to retire in Arizona, which is great for them, but unfortunately I don't see them as often as I should."

Secretly pleased he was opening up about his family, she responded in kind. "I don't see my parents much either, but for different reasons. My parents split up when I was young, and I bounced back and forth between households until I was sixteen, when I finally put my foot down and insisted on staying with my mother. It was awkward, especially after they both remarried."

She tensed a bit when Simon rested his hand in the small of her back. The way he was always touching her caught her off guard. Andrew hadn't been one to display overt gestures of affection. She couldn't deny how she loved the way Simon touched her, with the barest hint of possessiveness.

"That must have been difficult for you," Simon murmured as they headed out of the restaurant and back out to his car. "Did both of your parents have more children?"

"Yes," she admitted. "I have three half-brothers and two half-sisters, but they're all much younger than I am."

"I bet that didn't help in making you feel welcome," he said astutely.

She wrinkled her nose. "Yeah, pretty much. Don't get me wrong, it wasn't as if I didn't have a good childhood, because I did. Yet once I moved out to attend college, I knew I'd never go back." Which was why she was teetering on the brink of debt now. Between the car accident and moving to Cedar Bluff to start over, she'd used up the majority of her savings.

Simon drove to her apartment, pulling into the parking lot and then glancing over at her, his expression uncertain. "I had a great time, Hailey, and I have to confess, I'm not ready for the evening to end."

She caught her breath at his frank admission. "I'm not ready for the evening to end, either. Do you want to come up for a bit?"

He stared at her for a long moment. "Yes. And I don't want you to be offended, but I have an overnight kit in the trunk."

Her jaw dropped open in surprise. An overnight kit? So he'd planned to spend the night with her again? She wasn't sure if she should be flattered or upset. So much for thinking that they should slow things down a bit. "I honestly don't know what to say," she admitted.

"Don't be mad," he said, opening the driver's-side door. "I wasn't taking anything for granted, Hailey. I only threw some things together because I was hoping and praying you'd invite me up."

She climbed out of the car and reached into the backseat for her crutches. "And if I hadn't?"

He paused and shrugged. "I would have understood. It's your decision, Hailey. I can't say I wouldn't be disappointed, but if you've changed your mind about this—about us—then I'll leave you alone."

The ball was in her court and for the life of her she couldn't remember why she'd thought it would be best to slow things down. Maybe keeping her relationship with Simon on a professional level at the hospital was more difficult than she'd imagined but wasn't being with him worth the effort?

Did she really want him to leave?

"Please don't go," she said, reaching out to him. He came closer and folded her into a warm embrace.

"Are you sure?" he murmured, trailing a string of hot kisses down the side of her neck. "If you need more time, I'll understand."

More time? Wasn't it a bit late for that? They'd already made love once and she desperately wanted to be with him again. Had she ever felt this insatiable need with Andrew? If she had, she didn't remember it.

Enough of punishing herself for the past. She wanted this. She wanted him.

"I'm sure. Come inside with me, Simon." She flashed him a cheeky grin. "And don't forget your overnight bag."

He held her purse for her as Hailey opened her apartment door and flipped on the lights. Simon followed right behind her, carrying his small duffel bag.

For a moment there he'd prayed he hadn't been overconfident in telling her about the overnight kit he'd packed. Thank heavens Hailey hadn't taken offense.

"I'll, uh, just be a few minutes," she said, heading

down the hall toward the bathroom. "Make yourself at home."

He took her at her word, heading into her bedroom, tossing his bag onto the closest chair and setting her purse on the bedside table. In his duffel he had a change of boxers, his shaving gear and, of course, condoms.

Hailey had told him she was on the Pill, but he wasn't about to take anything for granted. Considering he didn't have to work until second shift the next day, he figured—or at least hoped—they could take their time and really enjoy themselves.

When Hailey emerged ten minutes later, dressed in a filmy nightgown that was so sheer it gave him an enticing view of her breasts, he nearly swallowed his tongue.

How had he gotten so lucky? Hailey was beautiful, sweet, sexy, smart and funny.

The whole package. Everything he'd always wanted in a woman. And more. For the first time in years he realized he could trust his gut instincts about her.

She wasn't Erica. Not by a long shot.

"You're so beautiful," he said as he crossed over to meet her. He tossed the crutches aside and gathered her into his arms. Lifting her up, he carried her to bed.

"So are you," she murmured, kissing his neck in a way that made him groan. She tugged at his shirt. "But I think you're overdressed."

"I think so too." He set her down and then quickly stripped off his clothes. As he joined her in bed, her cell phone rang.

"Ignore it," he whispered, suckling a rosy-tipped breast.

She gasped and arched beneath his kiss. "Okay."

He lifted up the sheer fabric, desperate to see all of her. Every glorious inch. And when her cell phone started ringing again, he swore under his breath and levered up to grab her purse with the phone inside and hand it to her. "Shut it off," he said huskily.

She chuckled and dug the cell phone out. She glanced at the screen. "That's odd," she murmured.

"What?" he could barely hide his impatience. He didn't care who was calling, he wanted to make love to Hailey. Now. Without any more interruptions.

"Both calls are from an unknown number," she said as she shut off the cell phone.

He froze, a chill running down the length of his spine. He swiftly took the phone from her hand, turned it back on and stared down at the screen.

The familiar words screamed at him.

Unknown number? Just like the non-stop hang-ups at both his home phone and his cell phone?

Dread twisted in his gut like a snake. This couldn't be a coincidence. All the calls had to be from the same person.

CHAPTER THIRTEEN

"Simon?" Hailey put a hand on his arm. "What is it?
What's wrong?"

He pulled his gaze up from the phone to look at her.
What should he tell her? He couldn't be certain who the
unknown caller was. Maybe the same telemarketers that
hounded him were bothering everyone that owned a cell
phone.

But even as the thought formed, he knew he was lying
to himself. There was no way the caller was a random
telemarketer.

Two years. He'd been in Cedar Bluff for *two years*.
Surely Erica had moved on by now. No woman in her
right mind would keep trying to track someone down
for two years.

But then again he couldn't say Erica had ever been in
her right mind. She was far from emotionally stable.

His fault. This was all his fault.

"Simon?" Hailey said again. "Tell me what's wrong."

He slowly shook his head, knowing he couldn't do
that. He couldn't explain and he definitely couldn't stay
to make love with Hailey.

"I'm sorry." Regretfully, he pulled the sheet up to

cover her bare breasts, before rolling off the bed and reaching for his discarded boxers. "I can't."

"What? You're leaving? *Now?*" Her incredulous tone made him wince and he felt a hundred times worse than she could ever know.

He was screwing this up badly, and he knew it. But he needed to know if he was just being paranoid or if it was even remotely possible that Erica was the one calling him.

Calling Hailey.

The hairs on the back of his neck lifted and the sick feeling in his gut twisted to the point that he almost doubled over in agony. How could Erica even know about Hailey? Even if she'd found his address and his phone number, he'd never once taken Hailey to his place.

Was Erica following him again? The way she had back in Chicago? And if so, why suddenly start calling Hailey?

Was she going to start stalking Hailey the way she'd continually come after him? And ruin her career as well?

The very thought made him want to slam his fist through the wall. None of this was Hailey's fault. None of it! Dammit, hadn't he suffered enough? What more did Erica want from him?

Whatever it was, maybe he deserved it, he thought with a tired sigh. But Hailey sure as hell didn't.

He glanced at Hailey, knowing he'd do anything to protect her. Because this was his mess to clean up, not hers. He needed to put an end to Erica's out-of-control behavior once and for all.

"I'm sorry," he said again, as he finished pulling on his clothes. "But I can't do this."

She wasn't about to let him off the hook so easily. "What can't you do? This? Us? Our relationship? Talk to me, Simon. You're not making any sense. I'm sure whatever the problem is, we can work it out. Together."

He reached for his duffel, steeling himself against the need to tell her everything. He shouldn't have let things go this far. Not until he'd dealt with Erica. Dragging Hailey into the mix wasn't fair.

How had he even thought he could have a future without settling the past, once and for all?

"I'm sorry," he repeated. "But I can't do this Hailey." Not yet anyway, he thought to himself.

Her gaze narrowed. "You're breaking up with me? Again? Just like that?"

"Yes." He forced himself to look her directly in the eye and lie. "This isn't working for me. I can't see you any more." The words felt like they had been wrenched out of him, each one more hurtful than the one before. But he was doing this to protect her. Because none of this was her fault.

"But—"

"Let's not make this worse than it already is. I made a mistake. I have to go." While she gaped at him, he quickly left, before she could say anything else.

And before he changed his mind.

Stunned, Hailey stared at the doorway long after Simon had closed it behind him.

Her thoughts swirled, a chaotic mass of confusion.

What had she done to push him away? What had caused Simon to swing from one extreme to the other?

He was the one who'd taken her out to dinner. He was the one who'd told her he didn't want the evening to end.

He was the one who'd packed an overnight bag!

Her heart squeezed in her chest, his words echoing over and over in her mind.

I made a mistake.

None of it made sense, but the loss devastated her. She buried her face in her hands, fighting tears.

She'd fallen in love with Simon. Forgiving herself for the accident had given her the freedom to fall in love. She loved Simon with a depth that she hadn't felt for Andrew.

But obviously Simon didn't feel the same way.

The ringing of her cell phone interrupted her pity-party. Sniffling, she reached for the instrument that Simon had tossed on the bed, suddenly hopeful. Was he calling her back to apologise? To explain he hadn't meant what he'd said?

Unknown number was displayed on her screen. Annoyed, she pushed the button to answer the call. "Hello?"

No response. But she could tell someone was on the other end of the line because she could hear breathing.

"Hello?" she said again. "Who is this?"

Still no response. She was just about to hang up when she finally heard a soft voice say, "Stay away from him."

"What?" Hailey wasn't sure she'd heard the female

caller correctly. At least, she thought it was a female caller. "Who is this? What do you want?"

"Stay away from him. Or else..."

The softly spoken warning sent a fissure of apprehension down her spine. "Or else what? Are you threatening me?"

She listened intently, but all she could hear was the sound of a dial tone buzzing loudly in her ear.

The caller had hung up.

Hailey flipped her phone shut, feeling more confused than ever. She'd never in her life been threatened. Stay away from him? From who? Simon?

Of course Simon. And suddenly she knew why Simon had left so abruptly. Why he'd broken up with her out of nowhere.

Because he knew who the unknown caller was.

His former girlfriend, Erica. The one who'd cost him his promising career at Children First in Chicago.

Erica must be here in Cedar Bluff. And she clearly wanted Simon back or she wouldn't have warned Hailey to stay away from him.

But the question remained. What did Simon want? Had he left her because he planned to go back to Erica?

Or because he'd given up on personal relationships for good?

Simon had stewed about the problem of Erica all night. And first thing in the morning, he'd known what he needed to do.

So he'd driven straight to the Cedar Bluff police station. But he hadn't gone in. Instead, he sat in the parking lot, inwardly debating the best course of action.

He closed his eyes and pressed his fingertips against his pounding temples. He knew his story would sound crazy. Totally nuts. Not to mention he had absolutely no proof, other than his gut instincts telling him that Erica had found him.

What could the police do with an unknown number? Probably not a hell of a lot.

Years ago, when he'd first realized Erica's attachment had grown to the level of stalking, he'd shied away from involving the authorities. Partially because he felt like an idiot. He'd been stupid enough to go out with her in the first place. And, besides, what guy couldn't handle a woman who'd become a little too attached? He'd thought he'd had everything under control. His pride had prevented him from asking for help. Instead, he'd kept trying to reason with her, over and over again.

But that approach hadn't worked.

So he'd simply done his best to avoid her, hoping the situation would resolve on its own. That she'd get tired of harassing him, coming over to confront him. Calling him.

And when that hadn't worked either, he'd picked up and moved his entire life, breaking off all his friendships, not telling anyone other than his parents where he'd gone. Cedar Bluff had been the perfect place to start over. Small enough and remote enough that Erica would never find him.

Maybe he should have called the police. But even then he'd known that Erica might have been arrested. And considering her fragile state, emotionally and physically, wasn't that adding insult to injury?

But now, two years later, the situation was well beyond the level of a nuisance.

For Hailey's sake, he needed to report it.

With renewed resolve he climbed from his car and strode into the police station. The place was buzzing with activity. He asked to speak to one of the detectives, and was taken over to a small office no bigger than a broom closet.

Detective Arnold had listened attentively while he'd explained the entire situation from start to finish. Even to his own ears, the story sounded unbelievable.

At least the detective hadn't laughed at him.

"So you think this unknown caller is this woman who's tracked you down over the course of two years?" Arnold said, summarizing his story in one sentence.

"Yeah. I do."

"Have you seen her in Cedar Bluff?" Detective Arnold asked.

"No. But I haven't seriously looked for her either," he admitted. Erica was pretty enough, with her shoulder-length dark brown hair and hazel eyes. She was rather tiny in stature, only five feet two inches tall and as thin as a rail. She wouldn't stand out as noticeable in the crowd unless you were looking for her.

The detective scratched his chin. "I guess we'll have to assume she's here somewhere. Unfortunately, women change their hair color on a whim, so your description of her isn't likely to do us any good. Maybe you've seen her but you just didn't recognize her?"

"Maybe." Simon had racked his brain all night,

trying to think of anyone he'd seen around his neighborhood who looked even remotely like Erica. There hadn't been anyone who'd even come close to fitting her description.

He'd wondered if Erica was working at Cedar Bluff, and had called the human resource office, asking about her, but he'd confirmed there were no nurses working at the hospital with that name. It wasn't likely Erica could fake a nursing license.

But maybe she was working in a nearby nursing home?

"We can put a trace on your home phone number," Arnold said, interrupting his thoughts. "But other than that, there isn't much we can do. You might want to consider changing your phone numbers."

Simon stared at the detective, his worst fears coming to fruition. "You need to understand, this woman is emotionally unbalanced. And she's calling Hailey Rogers, the woman I'm—er—was dating."

Arnold spread his hands helplessly. "Until you can give me something more to go on—a car, a place where you think she's staying, something concrete—there's nothing more I can do."

"What about searching all the hospitals, clinics and nursing homes in the area to see if she's working there as a nurse?"

The detective tapped his pencil on the table, looking thoughtful. Then he jotted down a few notes and slowly nodded. "Yeah, I can make a few phone calls. But in the meantime I suggest you pay attention to your surroundings. My guess is that she's somewhere close by, watching you."

Yeah. That's exactly what he was afraid of. Simon let his breath out in a heavy sigh. "Okay, thanks. If I do see her, I'll be sure to let you know."

"You do that," Arnold said as Simon stood and walked toward the door. "And you might want to warn your lady-friend, too."

Simon paused, swinging back to face the detective as the implication of that statement took a moment to sink into his brain.

Arnold was right. He shouldn't have left Hailey without explaining what was going on. If Erica had gone so far as to call Hailey, there was no telling what else she'd do. He'd been so panicked by the thought of Hailey being affected by this mess that he hadn't been thinking clearly.

"I will. Please let me know if you find anything out about Erica, too."

"I'll be in touch."

Satisfied he'd done what he could, Simon left the police station and walked outside into the bright sunlight. He paused and slid his sunglasses on, sweeping a gaze around to see if he saw anyone. Of course there was no one in sight. Shaking his head at his stupidity, he slid into the driver's seat of his car and headed back to the other side of town, toward Hailey's apartment building.

He needed to take the detective's advice to warn Hailey.

Simon pulled into the parking lot of Hailey's apartment building, once again glancing around curiously as he walked up to the door.

Being on edge like this was already driving him nuts.

He pushed the buzzer for Hailey's apartment and waited for her to respond.

He hit the buzzer again and again, still with no response. The manager of the apartment building came out to get his newspaper, saw Simon standing there and opened the door. "Can I help you?"

"Have you seen Hailey Rogers in apartment 211?" Simon asked.

"She left about twenty minutes ago, wearing scrubs, so I think she was planning to go to work," the elder man informed him.

"Okay, thanks." Simon headed back out to his car, glancing at his watch. Ten in the morning. How long would it take her to walk to the bus stop? Would she still be there?

He drove the couple of blocks to the bus stop, disappointed to find that Hailey wasn't sitting there, waiting. Maybe she was already at the hospital. For all he knew, she'd gone in early.

He relaxed, the tension easing out of his shoulders. The hospital was probably the safest place for Hailey right now. At least at work she was surrounded by plenty of people.

Besides, he sincerely doubted Erica would go as far as to attempt to harm Hailey. More likely she'd just continue to call her, doing nothing more than being a general pain in the ass. Erica was obsessed with him, not with Hailey.

He pulled over to the curb and called the hospital, asking to speak with Theresa. When the emergency department manager answered the phone, he quickly identified himself. "I hate to bother you, but would you

mind telling me what time Hailey came in this morning?" he asked. "I want to come in to work on some
paperwork, but wanted to wait until Hailey was finished
with my office."

"Ah, sure, let me see what time she swiped in." He
could hear the click of the keyboard as Theresa worked
on the computer. "I'm sorry, Simon, but Hailey hasn't
punched in for her shift yet."

"Oh, okay." Now he really felt like an idiot. "I must
have just missed her. Sorry to bother you."

"No problem. Bye, Simon."

He snapped his phone shut and drove home. He had
a few hours yet before he needed to pick up Hailey from
work. In the meantime, he planned to make a few phone
calls himself.

Maybe he'd find Erica before Detective Arnold did.

After a restless night of broken sleep, Hailey had decided to go into work early, so that she could get her
four hours of light-duty work out of the way before she
confronted Simon.

It wasn't until she'd arrived at the hospital that she'd
realized she wasn't sure what to work on as she'd been
doing his quality review project.

She walked over to Theresa's office, poking her head
in just as she hung up the phone. "Theresa? Do you
have the list of chart audits you wanted for the joint
commission?"

"Hailey, you startled me." Theresa put a hand over
her heart. "That was Simon on the phone, asking if you
were here. I told him you hadn't punched in yet."

Was Simon checking up on her? Because he was

concerned about her? Hope lightened her heavy heart. "Really? Did he ask to talk to me?"

"No, he just wanted to know what hours you were working so he'd know when he could get into his office." Theresa rummaged around on the messy piles of paper scattered across her desk. "Here's the list. Do you have a key to Simon's office?"

"No, I don't." She took the list of charts, stung by the knowledge that Simon wasn't concerned. Rather, he was trying to avoid her. "But it's no big deal, I'll find somewhere else to work."

"Okay. Good work on the quality reviews, by the way," Theresa said as she turned to leave. "Simon showed me your results and I think you're right on. We're going to discuss the signs and symptoms of sepsis at the next staff meeting. And Simon has already sent the same message out to all the physicians."

"Great, I'm glad I could help." Despite her sorrow over her break-up with Simon, Hailey was pleased that she'd been able to contribute to the unit, even in a small way.

"You have. And if you get all those audits done too, I'll be grateful. We expect the joint commission to show up in the next few weeks. If there are gaps in our documentation, I'd like to know about it now."

Hailey smiled. "I'll get them done," she promised.

When she walked out to the arena, the activity level was as high as usual. Remembering the last time she'd tried to work in the midst of the chaos, she decided to find the quietest work station she could.

She settled on the tiny computer workstation that was usually used by the ED educator. Since Joanne wasn't around, she figured no one would care if she used it. She could always move if Joanne needed her computer.

The chart audits were painstakingly slow, much worse than the quality reviews she'd completed for Simon. Her mind kept wandering, replaying those moments when Simon had broken things off. The more she thought about it, the more she became determined to confront him about his actions.

She realized, she hadn't really confronted Andrew about his actions until that fateful night. And, really, his drinking had been bothering her for weeks before that.

She needed to learn from her past mistakes once and for all. Why wait? The sooner she could talk to Simon, the sooner she could get to the bottom of what was going on. Besides, she was exhausted. Her lack of sleep was already causing her eyes to burn with gritty fatigue, the words on the computer screen reduced to a senseless blur.

She rubbed her eyes and pushed away the keyboard. There was no point in trying to work today. Not until she'd ironed out this issue with Simon. She could make up the hours tomorrow, as long as she didn't go over the amount that Theresa had approved.

Satisfied, she felt energised by her course of action. She would find Simon, and she would confront him about Erica. It couldn't be a coincidence that the moment her phone had rung, he'd suddenly changed his mind about being with her.

He must have broken things off because he was avoiding relationships altogether. But it was too late. They were already in a relationship.

She just needed to make him see that as well.

She walked into the female staff locker room to get her purse. Leaning on her crutches, she quickly opened her locker, took out her purse and shut the door.

When she turned, Mary, the unit clerk with the bleach blonde spiky hair and the freaky green eyes, was standing in front of the door. Hailey was surprised as she hadn't heard her come in. "Hi, Mary. What's up?"

The clerk stared at her across the room, without smiling. "I tried to warn you. You should have stayed away from him."

Dear heaven. A sick feeling curled in her stomach as realisation dawned. "Erica?"

"Yes. My real name is Erica. Mary is my sister. She let me borrow her identity so I could get this job. Wasn't that nice of her?"

Hailey stared at the woman blocking the doorway, all the seemingly insignificant details suddenly falling into place. "You bumped Bonnie, causing her to spill water in my lap on purpose," she accused. "Did you take the report from Simon's desk? And leave water on the floor? That last stunt was risky—you're lucky I didn't seriously hurt myself."

"I tried to warn you." Mary's expression didn't show one iota of remorse. "You were supposed to stay away from Simon."

Hailey sucked in a harsh breath when Mary, or rather Erica, reached behind to lock the door.

CHAPTER FOURTEEN

HAILEY swallowed nervously and watched Erica warily, trying to assess her options. The woman was blocking the doorway, but surely there was no reason to panic. Someone would come into the locker room sooner or later. Erica couldn't possibly keep her locked in here indefinitely.

Could she?

Obviously, this woman had seen her and Simon together. All the way back to that day he'd hit her bicycle and had then had stayed by her side, holding her hand.

She almost winced, realizing how much that would have bothered Erica.

But she wasn't going to apologise. Not for being with Simon. Or for loving him.

"What do you want, Erica?" Hailey finally asked, leaning heavily on her crutches. Maybe she could bluff her way out of this mess. "You want me to stay away from Simon? Okay, fine. He broke up with me anyway, so you have nothing to worry about."

Erica's blank, emotionless expression was eerie, to say the least. She just kept staring, acting as if she hadn't heard a word Hailey said. The weirdness of the entire situation was starting to get to her.

"Did you hear me?" Hailey said impatiently, in an attempt to break through the other woman's iron mask of indifference. "Simon is all yours! Take him with my blessing."

Another long pause. "We had a baby together. Did you know that? Did Simon tell you about our son?"

A son? Hailey couldn't prevent her jaw from dropping in shock. A baby? Simon hadn't said a word about a baby. "No, I'm afraid he didn't."

Erica reached into her scrub pocket, pulling out a small photograph. She smoothed the crumpled edges with her fingertips in a slow, overly deliberate way that suggested she performed the task often. "I have a picture. Do you want to see him?"

Hailey almost started to shake her head as she was still struggling with the idea of Simon and this woman having a baby together, but she sensed that making Erica more upset wasn't going to help. She'd already pretended she didn't care one bit about Simon. Maybe she needed to play along with this, too.

The sooner this poor woman got everything out of her system, the sooner they'd get out of the claustrophobic locker room. "Sure."

Erica held up the photograph. It was a grainy picture of a sonogram with the barest outline of a fetus. "See? Isn't he beautiful?"

"Ah, yes. He is. Beautiful," Hailey murmured, glancing briefly down at Erica's non-pregnant stomach. Was it remotely possible Erica was pregnant now? No, more likely she'd been pregnant in the past while she'd gone out with Simon.

Nothing in the world would make her believe Simon had been with Erica three months ago.

"His name is Joshua, just like Simon's father." Erica turned the photograph around and stared at it again for several long minutes. "Joshua Simon Carter," she murmured.

The way Erica was talking about the fetus, as if it were still alive, gave her the creeps. "That's a wonderful name. I'm sure Simon was very proud."

"Yes." She carefully tucked the photo in the pocket of her scrubs.

"Does Simon know you're here?" Hailey asked cautiously. "Have you spoken to him?"

"Not yet." A scowl crossed her features but then disappeared so quickly Hailey wondered if she'd imagined it. "He didn't recognize me because I've changed my hair color, eye color and padded my underwear. But I know he'll be glad to see me once he realizes it's me."

Hailey wasn't sure what to say about that. Her only option at this point was to agree with Erica, no matter how much she wanted to stake a claim in Simon for herself. "I'm sure he will."

"I'm glad you understand. Because Simon and I are going to have another baby together. To make up for the son we lost."

"I'm sorry for your loss, Erica." Hailey couldn't imagine how awful it must have been for Erica to lose the baby she'd obviously wanted very much. No wonder the woman had gone a little crazy. Could she really blame her?

"Oh, yes." Surprisingly, Erica nodded, and pulled out a syringe filled with a clear substance topped with a needle. "I do believe you will be sorry, Hailey. Very sorry that you had the audacity to come between me and Simon."

Simon spent a good two hours trying to find out if Erica was working as a nurse somewhere close to Cedar Bluff. But he soon gave up in frustration.

Because the more he spoke to the various human resources departments of the medical facilities he'd pinpointed as possibilities within a thirty-mile radius, the more he believed he was searching in vain.

What if Erica wasn't working as a nurse, especially since she'd need to go through the hassle of obtaining a Wisconsin nursing license? Erica could just as easily be working in some other capacity.

Hell, she could be a waitress or bartender for all he knew.

He glanced at his phone, wishing the detective would call with some news. And when he found himself glancing at the clock for the tenth time in half as many minutes, he gave up any pretense of working. He headed out to his car, determined to go to Cedar Bluff hospital to find Hailey.

He really needed to tell her the entire story about Erica. Something he should have done a long time ago.

When he arrived at the hospital, he strode quickly through the arena, searching for Hailey amidst the chaos. His office door was closed, and he grimaced as he realized he hadn't given Hailey his key.

He caught sight of Theresa and hurried over. "Where's Hailey?"

"I don't know, Simon. She was here a couple of hours ago. It seems our new unit clerk disappeared too, so if you find Hailey, see if she's willing to sit and answer phones for a while."

"Where was she working?" he asked, glancing around again, not seeing her at any of the workstations in the arena.

"Honestly, I have no clue." Theresa flashed him a harried smile before crossing over to answer a ringing phone. "Emergency Department, may I help you?"

He couldn't believe he'd missed Hailey. By his estimation, she should have at least another hour and a half of work yet to complete her allotted four hours. Perplexed, he crossed over to the locker room, thinking she was taking a break. When he tried the handle, he discovered the door was locked. "Hailey? Are you in there?"

"Simon?" He thought he heard Hailey cry out his name, but then there was the sound of a scuffle followed by a loud thud.

"Hailey!" Extremely worried now, he pounded on the door and tried the door handle again. "Open up!"

"I'm sorry, Simon." A sing-song voice that definitely wasn't Hailey. "I'm afraid Hailey is indisposed at the moment. You'll have to settle for me."

In that second he remembered what Theresa had said about the unit clerk disappearing. The new one? What was her name? Mary? With the bleached blonde short spiky hair? And the colored contact lenses?

No, not Mary. Erica. Dammit, he should have figured it out, despite the drastic differences. He'd never looked twice at the unit clerk, honestly hadn't paid the woman the least bit of attention.

He never should have assumed, even for a moment, that Erica would take a job somewhere else rather than here at the hospital.

He pulled out his cell phone and called Detective Arnold. Thankfully, the detective answered on the first ring. "Erica's here at Cedar Bluff hospital and she has Hailey locked in the woman's locker room."

"I'll send a team right away."

Simon snapped his phone shut and tried to think of what to do next. He wasn't going to attempt to reason with Erica, since that had never worked in the past. Better to find Theresa and someone from Security.

He had to get a key for the locker room.

"Simon? Are you still out there?" Erica called.

He'd managed to flag down Theresa, without going too far away. "Get Security up here with a master key, stat," he whispered urgently. In a louder voice he responded to Erica. "Yes, Erica, I'm here. Why don't you open the door so we can talk?"

"I told Hailey all about our son, Simon. She understands why you can't stay with her now."

This was nothing he hadn't heard before, but somehow knowing Hailey was locked inside made the entire situation much worse. Erica's miscarriage had been awful. He'd mourned the loss of their baby, too. He never should have left the birth-control responsibility to Erica alone. And then the miscarriage had sent Erica over the edge.

In the past, whenever Erica had talked crazily like this, he'd gently tried to ground her in reality.

But right now it seemed better to play along. No matter how much it pained him. "I broke up with Hailey," he told Erica. "I'm ready to get back together with you. Open the door, Erica. Please?"

"You are?" The cautious hopefulness in Erica's tone made him feel lower than sludge for raising her hopes, even for a moment. "Really?"

He closed his eyes and rested his forehead on the cold wooden door. "Yes. Open up, Erica. You don't need Hailey. Let's go away and talk, just the two of us. Alone."

Erica didn't respond right away, and he was getting more and more worried, especially when he couldn't hear Hailey. What had happened in there? Where in the hell was Security with that master key?

The seconds ticked by with excruciating slowness until finally a tall, dark-haired security officer came up behind him, waving a key.

Simon put a finger up to his lips, indicating the security guard should remain silent. The guy nodded to indicate he understood. Slowly, he slid the key into the lock.

The guard met his gaze questioningly, and Simon nodded. "Go!"

The guard twisted the key and threw his weight into the act of opening the door in case Erica had blocked it with something heavy on the other side. The door opened surprisingly easily, but when he came in behind the security guard, he saw Hailey crumpled on the floor, her casted leg stuck out at an awkward angle.

"Simon!" Erica cried as she rushed toward him.

Thankfully the security guard caught her before she

reached Simon and quickly grabbed hold of her wrists. "Ma'am, you need to come with me."

"No!" Erica screamed, struggling against the security guard. "Simon!"

He flicked her a brief glance, feeling nothing but pity for her, before he knelt beside Hailey. "Hailey? Wake up, honey. Are you all right?"

At the sound of his voice, her eyelids fluttered open. She tried to say something, but he couldn't make it out. Her eyelids drifted back down.

Had she hit her head? He was about to lift her head to examine it for wounds when he spied the needle and syringe on the floor.

Dear God. *Erica had drugged Hailey!*

Simon sat beside Hailey's bedside, his head bowed over their clasped hands, listening to the reassuring sounds of the dialysis machine and the heart monitor beeping over her head. Jadon had told him she'd be fine, but he wouldn't believe it until she woke up.

Detective Arnold had arrived and arrested Erica. Simon knew he should have gotten the police involved much earlier.

Like two years ago, when she'd vandalised his car.

And had started following him everywhere, calling him day and night. Begging to have another baby with him.

His stupid pride had nearly cost Hailey her life. Erica had given her enough of the drug to stop her breathing. Luckily, they'd caught her before her respiratory rate had fallen too low.

He never should have left her last night. Hailey hadn't done anything wrong. She didn't deserve this.

When Hailey stirred, tugging at his hand, his head shot up, his gaze searching her face. "Hailey? Are you all right?"

"Simon?" she frowned and glanced around the room in confusion. "Where am I?"

One side effect of Versed, the drug Erica had used, was an amnesic affect. "You're in the hospital, getting dialysis. Do you remember being locked in with Erica?"

Instantly her confusion cleared. "Yes." With her free hand she reached for a cup of water, taking a long sip before resting back against the pillow with a sigh. "She told me about the baby."

Cautiously, he nodded. "I didn't know she was pregnant when I broke off our relationship, Hailey. She was so clingy, so needy, constantly going wherever I was, calling me non-stop. But I swear to you I didn't know she was pregnant. And when she told me she was expecting our child, I agreed to support her and the baby financially. I wanted to be a part of my child's life. But she would settle for nothing less than marriage."

He paused as memories of the past clouded his mind. Especially the deep fear that Erica would take off with his child and disappear. "When I told her I wasn't going to marry her, she went a little crazy. She took a steel-pronged rake to my car, gouging the hell out of it. I should have called the police then, but she was pregnant with my child. I couldn't do that to her. Not when her pregnancy was as much my responsibility as hers. So instead I kept trying to reason with her, even though she kept insisting that we had to be a family." He scrubbed a hand over his face in a weak attempt to erase the past.

"What happened then?" Hailey asked.

"I was working when she called me, completely hysterical, crying because she was bleeding." For several seconds he stared at their clasped hands, before dragging his resigned gaze up to hers. "She lost the baby. I couldn't believe how much that loss hurt. Yet as bad as I felt about losing the baby, I can't deny I was also a little bit relieved. For her sake, more than anything. I figured losing the baby was somehow meant to be. I thought she'd be able to move on with her life. Make a fresh start. But unfortunately losing the baby only pushed her further over the edge of sanity."

"So she started stalking you."

Even now, after all this time, he shied away from the ugly term. But he couldn't deny the truth. Lying to himself about the seriousness of Erica's obsession was how Hailey had ended up on the wrong side of a hospital bed.

"Yeah. She began stalking me. Kept showing up at my house, at work, at the gym, begging me to take her back, to make another baby." He sighed. "It was awful. After the big scene in the middle of the emergency department, when she literally attacked me physically, I took the easy way out. I packed my gear, quit my job and moved out of Chicago." At the time he'd thought he was doing the right thing. "But what I should have done was reported her to the police. I'm sorry, Hailey. I'm so sorry you had to go through that."

"Yeah, I wouldn't recommend it." She gave a wry smile and shifted restlessly on the bed. "But you know—I don't hate Erica. I actually felt sorry for her, Simon."

He couldn't hide his surprise. "Even after she locked you up and drugged you?"

Hailey grimaced. "Well, not that part so much. But I'm sure losing the baby was hard on her. And I think, in her own way, she really did love you."

Simon slowly shook his head. "No, you're wrong about that, Hailey. She was only in love with some fabricated image of what she wanted me to be. That's one of the things I regret the most. I knew, almost from the beginning, that things weren't going to work out between us, but I allowed our relationship to get intimate. That was one of my biggest mistakes."

"Don't torture yourself, Simon," Hailey murmured, turning his own words to her during their dinner at Stephen's against him. "You can't play the what-if game, remember?"

He refused to be sidetracked. "I'm surprised you don't resent Erica for what she's done. You're an amazing woman, Hailey."

"You're not so bad yourself, Simon," she said, flashing a sleepy smile, her eyelids sliding closed.

He loosened his grip on her hand, intending to leave her to recover in peace, but her eyes flew open the moment he let go. "Where are you going?"

"I thought maybe you'd rather be alone." He wouldn't blame her for not wanting to see him, a constant reminder of the horror she'd gone through.

She clung to his hand, her glassy gaze focused on his. "Were you serious last night, when you said our relationship was over?"

His heart swelled with hope at the uncertainty in her gaze. "No, Hailey. That was just a misguided attempt to spare you from all this…" He waved a hand in disgust. He tried to read her facial expression. "Are you telling me that after everything that's happened, you're still willing to give me a second chance?"

"Do you want a second chance?" she asked, instead of answering his question.

"Yes, Hailey. God yes." He pulled her hand up and pressed a kiss in the center of her palm. "When I saw you lying on the floor, I was afraid I hadn't arrived in time." He took a deep breath and decided to bare his soul. "I love you, Hailey. More than you can possibly know."

Her eyes widened at his declaration. "You do?"

"Yes. I do." Just saying the words gave him a sense of freedom. For too long he'd refused to let anyone get close. Had been afraid of commitment. And the possibility of a family.

Now, Hailey could never be close enough. "I think I knew, right from the start, that we were meant to be together. But I understand if you need time to get used to the idea," he added when she didn't say anything more. "Take as much time as you need. But know this, Hailey. I'll be ready and waiting for you, no matter how long it takes. I'm in this for the long haul. There's no rush. We have plenty of time."

Hell, was he babbling?

He seriously needed to get a grip.

"That's very sweet, Simon, but I don't need any time. I already know how I feel." Her mouth curved into a sweet smile and yet he found himself holding his breath, almost afraid to hope. "I love you, too."

"Oh, Hailey." He bent over the bed and gathered her as close as the dialysis machine would allow. He buried his face in her hair, knowing he was the luckiest man alive. "You've forgiven me way too easily."

She let out a muffled laugh. "Oh, yeah? Are you complaining?"

"Never," he vowed. "I swear I'll make it up to you."

"Ah, Simon." She lifted her face and gently kissed him. "Don't you know? You already have."

EPILOGUE

HAILEY rejoiced with a little skip as she started up the steps to her apartment on the second floor, her first time since getting the bulky cast off her leg.

Freedom! Who would have thought that walking up stairs could be so fabulous?

Her cell phone rang and she knew the caller was Simon before she glanced at the screen. He'd already surprised her with a brand-new bicycle, to replace the one he'd crunched under his bumper. She'd taken her first ride on it today, while he was finishing up his day shift.

"Hi, Simon."

"Hailey, we're celebrating tonight, so put on your dancing shoes and be ready by six."

Even though he couldn't see her, she raised her hand in a mock salute. "Yes, sir."

He chuckled. "Okay, sorry. I didn't mean that to sound like an order."

"I know." She giggled as she put the key in her lock and opened her apartment door. "Don't worry. I'll be ready by six. Where are you taking me?"

"It's a surprise."

Her grin widened. "I love surprises." And she had

a surprise for Simon too. She was ready to get behind the wheel of a car. She'd been practicing, without his knowing. She couldn't wait to tell him.

Hailey took her time, lingering in a bubble bath that was nothing short of heavenly. Her right leg looked a little pale and small compared to her left, but she didn't care. She pulled on the slinkiest red dress she owned and was ready and waiting when Simon showed up.

He whistled when he saw her, frank admiration in his gaze. "You look amazing."

"Thanks, so do you." His dark shirt and slacks were casually elegant. He was by far the most handsome guy in the universe, in her opinion.

Simon drove to a restaurant on the outskirts of town, and she could hear the band playing from the parking lot. The thought of dancing with Simon made her pulse skip with excitement.

She barely had time to put her purse on the chair before he was tugging on her hand, drawing her out onto the dance floor. She would have sworn he'd paid the guy off, because the music immediately slowed to an intimate pace. When he stroked his hand down her back, lingering low on her waist, she shivered.

They danced three songs in a row, before he deemed it break time and escorted her over to a cozy table off to the side.

She tensed, just for a moment, when the waiter came over, but once again, Simon told him they'd stick with water. "Go ahead and bring out the first course," he said.

The waiter bowed and disappeared.

She flashed him a mock frown. "What's the first

course? Don't I have a choice as to what I want to eat?"

Simon shrugged. "You always have a choice, Hailey. Wait to see what it is first, and if you don't like it, we'll send it back to the kitchen for something else."

She sighed, reminding herself that she loved surprises. She took a sip of her water, gazing at Simon. He was so handsome he made her heart ache. The past five weeks with him had been wonderful.

"Thank you, Simon. This is the perfect way to celebrate getting my cast off."

"You're welcome, Hailey."

At that moment, the waiter came out with one silver-dome-covered tray that he set in front of Hailey.

"Don't you get one?" she asked.

Simon gave a tiny shake of his head, his gaze surprisingly wary. "I'll share yours."

The waiter paused dramatically, and then lifted the cover. Instead of a mouth-watering appetizer, a small black velvet ring box sat on the middle of the plate.

She sucked in a quick breath, raising a shocked gaze to Simon. "What is this?"

He looked tense, his gaze searching hers as he said, "Open it."

With fingers that threatened to tremble, she picked up the box and opened it. A beautiful emerald-cut diamond glittered inside. "Oh, Simon!"

"Hailey, will you marry me?"

Tears threatened, and she blinked them away furiously. They'd only been together for six weeks, but she didn't for one minute doubt her feelings for him.

Or his feelings for her.

"Yes, Simon. I'd be honored." And since she wasn't hampered by her cast any longer, she picked up the ring and jumped up from the table, and went over to wrap her arms around him in an exuberant hug.

He took the ring and slid it onto the third finger of her left hand. "Come on," he murmured, nudging her once again toward the dance floor where the music instantly turned to a slow, romantic number. He'd definitely paid off the band leader.

"I'd like to dance with my fiancée," he murmured softly, nuzzling her ear.

"For the rest of our lives," Hailey agreed with a sigh as she rose up on her tiptoes and captured his mouth in a heartfelt kiss.

MILLS & BOON

FEBRUARY 2011 HARDBACK TITLES

ROMANCE

Flora's Defiance	Lynne Graham
The Reluctant Duke	Carole Mortimer
The Wedding Charade	Melanie Milburne
The Devil Wears Kolovsky	Carol Marinelli
His Unknown Heir	Chantelle Shaw
Princess From the Past	Caitlin Crews
The Inherited Bride	Maisey Yates
Interview with a Playboy	Kathryn Ross
Walk on the Wild Side	Natalie Anderson
Do Not Disturb	Anna Cleary
The Nanny and the CEO	Rebecca Winters
Crown Prince, Pregnant Bride!	Raye Morgan
Friends to Forever	Nikki Logan
Beauty and the Brooding Boss	Barbara Wallace
Three Weddings and a Baby	Fiona Harper
The Last Summer of Being Single	Nina Harrington
Single Dad's Triple Trouble	Fiona Lowe
Midwife, Mother…Italian's Wife	Fiona McArthur

HISTORICAL

Miss in a Man's World	Anne Ashley
Captain Corcoran's Hoyden Bride	Annie Burrows
His Counterfeit Condesa	Joanna Fulford
Rebellious Rake, Innocent Governess	Elizabeth Beacon

MEDICAL™

Cedar Bluff's Most Eligible Bachelor	Laura Iding
Doctor: Diamond in the Rough	Lucy Clark
Becoming Dr Bellini's Bride	Joanna Neil
St Piran's: Daredevil, Doctor…Dad!	Anne Fraser

FEBRUARY 2011 LARGE PRINT TITLES

ROMANCE

The Reluctant Surrender	Penny Jordan
Shameful Secret, Shotgun Wedding	Sharon Kendrick
The Virgin's Choice	Jennie Lucas
Scandal: Unclaimed Love-Child	Melanie Milburne
Accidentally Pregnant!	Rebecca Winters
Star-Crossed Sweethearts	Jackie Braun
A Miracle for His Secret Son	Barbara Hannay
Proud Rancher, Precious Bundle	Donna Alward

HISTORICAL

Lord Portman's Troublesome Wife	Mary Nichols
The Duke's Governess Bride	Miranda Jarrett
Conquered and Seduced	Lyn Randal
The Dark Viscount	Deborah Simmons

MEDICAL™

Wishing for a Miracle	Alison Roberts
The Marry-Me Wish	Alison Roberts
Prince Charming of Harley Street	Anne Fraser
The Heart Doctor and the Baby	Lynne Marshall
The Secret Doctor	Joanna Neil
The Doctor's Double Trouble	Lucy Clark

MARCH 2011
HARDBACK TITLES

ROMANCE

A Stormy Spanish Summer	Penny Jordan
Taming the Last St Claire	Carole Mortimer
Not a Marrying Man	Miranda Lee
The Far Side of Paradise	Robyn Donald
Secrets of the Oasis	Abby Green
The Proud Wife	Kate Walker
The Heir From Nowhere	Trish Morey
One Desert Night	Maggie Cox
Her Not-So-Secret Diary	Anne Oliver
The Wedding Date	Ally Blake
The Baby Swap Miracle	Caroline Anderson
Honeymoon with the Rancher	Donna Alward
Expecting Royal Twins!	Melissa McClone
To Dance with a Prince	Cara Colter
Molly Cooper's Dream Date	Barbara Hannay
If the Red Slipper Fits...	Shirley Jump
The Man with the Locked Away Heart	Melanie Milburne
Socialite...or Nurse in a Million?	Molly Evans

HISTORICAL

More Than a Mistress	Ann Lethbridge
The Return of Lord Conistone	Lucy Ashford
Sir Ashley's Mettlesome Match	Mary Nichols
The Conqueror's Lady	Terri Brisbin

MEDICAL™

Summer Seaside Wedding	Abigail Gordon
Reunited: A Miracle Marriage	Judy Campbell
St Piran's: The Brooding Heart Surgeon	Alison Roberts
Playboy Doctor to Doting Dad	Sue MacKay

0211 Gen Std LP

MARCH 2011
LARGE PRINT TITLES

ROMANCE

The Dutiful Wife	Penny Jordan
His Christmas Virgin	Carole Mortimer
Public Marriage, Private Secrets	Helen Bianchin
Forbidden or For Bedding?	Julia James
Christmas with her Boss	Marion Lennox
Firefighter's Doorstep Baby	Barbara McMahon
Daddy by Christmas	Patricia Thayer
Christmas Magic on the Mountain	Melissa McClone

HISTORICAL

Reawakening Miss Calverley	Sylvia Andrew
The Unmasking of a Lady	Emily May
Captured by the Warrior	Meriel Fuller
The Accidental Princess	Michelle Willingham

MEDICAL™

Dating the Millionaire Doctor	Marion Lennox
Alessandro and the Cheery Nanny	Amy Andrews
Valentino's Pregnancy Bombshell	Amy Andrews
A Knight for Nurse Hart	Laura Iding
A Nurse to Tame the Playboy	Maggie Kingsley
Village Midwife, Blushing Bride	Gill Sanderson